# KRAEV

WARRIORS OF RAE – BOOK 1

STARR HUNTRESS

SONIA NOVA

# KRAEV

www.starrhuntress.com
www.sonianova.com

## THE STORY SO FAR

When aliens arrived on Earth, it happened with an invasion – just like the sci-fi movies taught us to expect.

The vicious Suhlik meant to enslave Earth and rob her of her resources. Only the Mahdfel warriors stood against them.

Once the slaves of the Suhlik, the Mahdfel won their freedom. But as a lingering reminder of their oppression at the hands of the Suhlik, they cannot have female children.

Now, in exchange for protecting Earth, the hunky alien warriors demand only one price: every childless, single and otherwise healthy woman on Earth is tested for genetic compatibility for marriage with a Mahdfel warrior. If the match is 98.5% or higher, the bride is instantly teleported away to her new mate.

No exceptions.

# 1

## OLIVIA

OLIVIA PRESSED the stethoscope on Mrs. Miller's back.

"Okay, Mrs. Miller. If you could just breathe deeply now..."

The older woman inhaled and Olivia listened to the raspy sound of her lungs pulling in air. Mrs. Miller was barely in her forties, but with the deep wrinkles on her face and tired eyes, she looked much older. The years since the Suhlik invasion on Earth nearly two decades ago had clearly not been kind to her.

As Olivia moved the stethoscope on the woman's back, the bracelet she always wore around her wrist fell past the sleeve of her shirt. She hurriedly pushed it back. Technically, she wasn't supposed to be wearing the thing while she was working in the hospital, but there was no way she was going to take it off until she was forced to.

"Do you hear it, Miss Griffin?" Dr. Malcom, her attending physician, asked behind her.

Mrs. Miller pulled in another ragged breath, and Olivia nodded to the doctor. She moved the stethoscope off Mrs. Miller's back and turned to face the woman.

"Mrs. Miller, I'm really sorry to say this but it seems that your condition has deteriorated since your last visit. I'm afraid the oxygen treatment has been ineffective."

Mrs. Miller smiled sadly. "I had thought as much."

"What do you suggest as the next step, Miss Griffin?" Dr. Malcom glanced at her. He was a kind and understanding doctor, sometimes strict with the medical students, but that only made him a better supervisor.

"I recommend moving on to an oxygen tank," Olivia said to Mrs. Miller, trying to keep herself calm. The weight of the bracelet on her wrist suddenly felt heavy. "The large tanks are not ideal as they are quite heavy to pull around, but at this point, you should have direct access to oxygen whenever you need it."

Mrs. Miller nodded grimly. "I understand."

"We will get you arranged with the equipment you need, Mrs. Miller," Dr. Malcom said. "Although no cure has been discovered for lung damage caused by the Suhlik gas attacks, regular intake of oxygen will help your breathing. Miss Griffin will help you sign the necessary papers to get the equipment."

"Thank you, doctor." Mrs. Miller rose from her seat slowly, as if the slight movement might already take the air from her lungs. Olivia forced her expression to remain neutral. None of the devastation she felt inside showed.

"Right this way, Mrs. Miller." She walked to the door and escorted the woman out. They walked slowly to the reception, with Mrs. Miller breathing heavily with every step.

A nurse took her information and Olivia explained Mrs. Miller's medical needs to her. They filled out the necessary forms together before the nurse brought out an oxygen tank for Mrs. Miller and she walked to the exit.

"Take care, Mrs. Miller," Olivia said.

"You too, my dear." Mrs. Miller smiled. "Thank you for taking such good care of me today and good luck with your medical studies. I know you will become a fine doctor one day."

A smile formed on Olivia's lips. "Thank you, Mrs. Miller."

Mrs. Miller walked out the automatic doors, pulling her new oxygen tank behind her, and Olivia let out a heavy sigh. These were always the worst situations as a doctor. When there was nothing you could do to help the inevitable.

Olivia cursed the Suhlik in her mind. The new illnesses that had developed after the lizard-like aliens attacked the planet had been the source of scores of academic papers, even entire medical journals. New illnesses were still revealing themselves, nearly two decades later.

And for most of them, there was no cure.

Yet, Olivia didn't doubt her conviction in wanting to become a doctor for even a second. She turned back toward Dr. Malcom's office, fiddling with the bracelet around her wrist. It had been her best friend, Tammy's. They'd lived right next door to each other and been friends since before either of them could remember. Doctors and nurses had been their favorite game.

Then… The Suhlik had come and everything had changed.

The tall, golden bodies of the lizards – so utterly beautiful and yet frightening at once – had beamed down onto the planet and gone on a massacre. Olivia and her family had survived by chance because they had been visiting her grandparents out of state and hadn't been at home.

Tammy and her family hadn't been so lucky.

Olivia had watched Tammy as she wilted and withered away over the three days after the attack on her city. Her tiny body had been unable to deal with the toxic effects of the Suhlik poison – the very same gas that was now slowly, over the years, deteriorating Mrs. Miller's lungs.

Within days, Tammy had given in, first to a coma and then to death. Before she passed, she'd given Olivia the bracelet she refused to take off her wrist. Tammy had told her that she wanted her to have it so that she could remember her.

As if she'd ever be able to forget.

Olivia took a deep breath, calming herself before she turned to enter Dr. Malcom's office. But before she could open the door, a male voice called out to her down the corridor.

"Miss Olivia Griffin?"

She turned on her heel and faced two soldiers holding assault rifles in their hands.

Olivia's heart immediately sunk. She knew what the men were here for.

Her time had come.

After the Suhlik attack, another alien race known

as the Mahdfel had come to Earth's defense. They had fought off the lizards with technology far beyond humanity's progress, but their aid hadn't been selfless. The Mahdfel had been genetically engineered by the Suhlik to be stronger and faster, but as a result of that, their ability to have female children had disappeared. So, they'd made agreements with other planets. Protection in exchange for females.

They had saved planet Earth and in return, they were now asking humanity to give them women so they could continue their race. And of course, in the face of extinction, the Earth governments had agreed.

Every single, childless, and healthy woman was now mandated by law to be tested for genetic compatibility with Mahdfel warriors. And if the compatibility was 98.5% or higher, they were immediately teleported to a Mahdfel-occupied planet to spend the rest of their life there as an alien's bride.

No exceptions.

Olivia had slipped through the cracks so far. She'd thought maybe someone was making sure that she didn't have to be tested. Doctors were in such short supply nowadays, even though they were needed more than ever. She was an asset to the state.

She'd thought maybe that would protect her, but apparently not.

It was time for her to find out whether she was compatible. Whether she was going to be shipped off to another world to leave her dreams and family behind.

In some states, the testing was done on birthdays – the ultimate birthday present, right? – and in others, a series of numbers were called every week like some depressing lottery. In Olivia's state, it was seemingly random. One day, soldiers showed up on your doorstep – or at work – and you were taken whether you wanted it or not.

If she resisted, she'd be forced anyway. That's what the guns were there for. And that's why they came at random: to prevent anyone from escaping if they knew about the testing in advance.

Olivia nodded to the soldiers. Really, she had no choice but to follow them out of the hospital. The soldiers guided her to a large van filled with other women who were mostly staring into space with dull looks in their eyes.

The stories were that being a Mahdfel bride was good. You lived a life of luxury with someone who adored you. At least, that was what the news said. She didn't trust any of the propaganda coming from the state that was forcing this on them in the first place. Of course, they weren't going to admit if the Mahdfel actually kept women locked up as sex slaves or something.

But there was one woman in the van who could barely keep the smile off her face.

At least someone had bought into the probable lies.

The van drove to the testing facility on the outskirts of the city. Deceptively, it looked like any other office building. There had been a lot of destruction when the lizards came, and a lot of rebuilding afterward. This was one of the new buildings that had gone up, and so it was ugly. Made of gray concrete, it was just the quickest and cheapest thing that could go up. It was fitting.

They unloaded from the van and walked into the testing building. The soldiers led them to a waiting room where they went one-by-one into a small office to get their fingers pricked and to find out within minutes whether their life was going to change forever.

Of course, the chances of being a match were minimal, but for the first time since she was old enough to understand such things, Olivia wished she'd more seriously considered getting married to another human. She was twenty-seven. She could have married someone. She could have been pregnant. That would have gotten her out of the testing now.

She was sure she could have found someone willing to make the sacrifice of marrying her so that she didn't have to face this situation. Her father had offered to search once. He desperately hadn't wanted her to end up where she was right now.

Tears stung in her eyes at the thought of never seeing her father again. Or her mother and younger brother. They had all been through so much, and now she might never even get to say goodbye. They'd get the money as compensation for her sudden departure, but that would be all.

"Miss Griffin?" Her stomach dropped when her name was called and she was brought back from her thoughts.

Slowly, she stood up from her seat, her whole body feeling numb as she walked to the testing room. The nurse inside was a middle-aged woman with a kind face. She smiled at Olivia and gestured for her to take a seat.

The friendliness of the nurse only made everything harder as she put out her finger for it to be pricked. She'd have preferred someone aggressive or harsh, not someone who looked like they pitied her.

She barely felt the needle as it pierced her skin

and a drop of blood collected on her fingertip. She stared at the wall to her side in silence. She didn't want to be a part of any of this. A million thoughts a second raced through her mind, all of them focused on the life she might be about to leave behind.

The minutes were agonizingly long as they waited for the results. And then…

"You're a match."

Olivia sucked in a breath. She felt the blood drain from her face and her whole body froze. She was so stiff she thought she might break in two.

"What?" she whispered, her voice oddly hoarse. "A match? That… that can't be right."

She'd been working herself up about the possibility, but it was never supposed to actually *happen*. This wasn't what her life was supposed to look like. She was supposed to go back to her life and her family and be outraged by the principle of it happening from the safety of her home. She was supposed to become *a doctor.*

"You are a genetic match with a Raewan-Mahdfel warrior named Kraev ek-Tayn," the nurse said, though Olivia barely heard it. Her blood pounded in her ears and her thoughts were moving a mile a minute.

Leave Earth. Go and be a baby-maker for an alien man she didn't even know…

"Miss Griffin?" the nurse said, leaning forward and putting a gentle hand on Olivia's shoulder. "Olivia… I understand this must come as a shock to you, but you are a match. The sooner you accept that, the better."

"I… I can't."

"Yes, you can."

Olivia shook her head, but she knew there was nothing she could do. No other option. She was a match. She was going to – where was she even going? She hadn't been listening to the nurse at all.

"Where am I going? Who is my match?" she asked.

The nurse didn't look exasperated as she repeated the information Olivia was sure she'd already given. "His name is Kraev ek-Tayn. He's a Raewan-Mahdfel. You'll be going to planet R-2841."

"R-2841?" Olivia blinked. "That's the name of the planet? It doesn't have… like a proper name?" Already, dread was settling in her stomach. What kind of backward planet was she going to that it didn't even have a name?

"That's all it says here, yes. Apparently, it's a mining colony in the same galaxy as your match's home planet, Raewan."

"A mining colony?" Olivia repeated in horror. She didn't want to go *anywhere*, but if she had to go somewhere, she would've at least liked to go somewhere… civilized. A planet filled with cities or some exotic new world. Not a nameless colony.

"How many people live on the planet? Is it even inhabitable?"

"I don't know how many people live there. There is an oxygen atmosphere. Believe me, you would not be sent anywhere unsafe."

The nurse pressed a button on her desk, and Olivia knew the guards would soon be here to pick her up to be teleported.

"Wait, I just want to say goodbye to my parents. My younger brother…"

"They'll understand what's happened."

"That's not good enough."

The door opened and two soldiers stood on the other side, waiting for her.

"You can give the money to them," the nurse said, holding up a tablet to her as if that would make it all better. The brides were each given a million dollars to grant their families or whoever they wanted as compensation for being forced off-planet and essentially into a life of slavery. "You can nominate up to five people to receive the money, and split it any way you want."

Olivia looked long and hard at the tablet. She had tried so hard to avoid thinking about the whole process that she'd never thought much about this part. Who would she give the money to?

Of course, her family would get most of it. She wrote her parents' and brother's names in the first boxes, and then chewed her lip on the amount.

In the end, she decided to give them each a quarter of the money. The rest she donated to a charity for which she'd campaigned ever since she was old enough. The charity did lots of research into the newly emerged Suhlik-influenced diseases, and they helped people cope with their diagnosis and the mental conditions brought on by the Suhlik attacks on the planet. They did incredible work, and Olivia knew her money couldn't have gone to a better cause.

She handed the tablet back to the nurse with her signature.

"Here," the nurse said, handing her a small sweet. "This mint will help with the teleportation-associated nausea. Take it as soon as you get to the other side of the teleport."

Olivia put it in her pocket. "Thank you."

"The last thing we need is to implant a translator," the nurse explained as one of the guards stepped in and retrieved a small case from a shelf. "If you could just hold your hair out of the way."

Olivia did as she was told, and the nurse

implanted the translator just behind her right ear. She expected to feel something, for there to be a sharp pain, but it was virtually painless. She wasn't even certain the nurse had implanted it until she was moving away from her again.

"It's time," one of the soldiers said behind her.

The nurse wished her good luck and the men escorted Olivia out of the room.

The urge to run away was overwhelming, but Olivia knew she'd have gotten about two feet before one of the soldiers stopped her. All that running would do was embarrass herself. She still took a step backward automatically as they reached the teleport room, and she felt the soldiers tense. She wondered how many people did run.

But the next step she took was forward. She walked past the soldiers and into the room where she'd disappear from Earth – possibly forever – with her head held high and almost managing to hide the tremors in her hands.

Inside the room was a huge cylindrical machine. A teleporter. She'd never seen one in person before, and once again wanted to back away from it like a scared little girl.

"Okay," one of the soldiers said, moving away from Olivia and standing at a control panel by the teleporter. "You'll just stand in the chamber, and I'll make the teleportation happen. You'll feel nauseous when you arrive at your destination, but the mint will help. The nausea will be worse the more you move, so I advise standing still."

Olivia nodded numbly. The room didn't even have windows. She wouldn't even get one last glimpse at the outside world before she was taken off the planet and sent to her new home. Her last image of Earth would be the nasty gray concrete of the office where her fate had been sealed.

It was almost enough to make her cry.

She walked into the chamber of the teleporter and closed her eyes as she listened to one of the soldiers tap on the controls.

And then, with a flash of light, she was off.

## 2

### KRAEV

KRAEV REACHED up and picked a piece of fruit from one of the trees in the greenhouse. This was his favorite place to spend his off-duty time on the barren and icy planet of R-2841. The greenhouses were huge domes on the surface of the planet that managed to stay warm despite the harsh environment, and they were filled with colorful plants from all over the universe. But most importantly, they produced fruits from his home planet, Raewan.

Despite the food replicators that could make him any meal in the known universe or even create fruit-imitations, those were nothing compared to picking something straight off the tree.

"I heard there was another Suhlik attack last

night," his friend, Zevyk, said as he walked up to Kraev.

Kraev bit into his fruit and swallowed before responding. "Yes. The arrogant lizards thought they could get on the surface. It was a full-frontal attack. Hundreds of Suhlik ships right outside the planet. I blew up at least a dozen of them."

Zevyk grinned. "I wish I had been there to see it. I had just finished my shift in the control room and was sleeping."

Kraev chuckled. "You didn't miss out on much. They were pathetic. I doubt they'll try again for a while." He paused, taking another bite of his fruit. "But I don't want to talk about Suhlik while I'm off-duty."

Zevyk picked a piece of fruit as well and sat down next to Kraev. The purple-and-blue *amihae* were delicious and reminded Kraev of their home. "What do you want to talk about then?"

"Anything. Like the pleasant weather of this planet."

Zevyk laughed now. Neither of them was particularly enamored with R-2841. It was a hostile and dangerous planet. But it was also vital to the Mahdfel.

Hellstone, an incredibly rare mineral, could be found in abundance in the volcanoes of R-2841. The mineral had a unique quality that could prevent teleportation, and it was important for the defense of any Mahdfel location. It was Kraev's duty as a pilot defending the planet to ensure that the Suhlik never gained control of the mines.

Among the warriors stationed on R-2841, the planet was affectionately nicknamed "hellhole" after hellstone and the barren landscape. The name was very fitting, which is why Kraev escaped to the greenhouses whenever he could.

"Well, I think the weather has been warming up the past few days," Zevyk said, a contemplative expression on his face. Kraev could tell his friend was joking, but he was probably the only one who could. Zevyk was often so serious that not many understood his dry sense of humor.

Kraev was about to make another witty remark about the weather, when a sudden beep and a flashing white light on his wristband interrupted their conversation.

*A new message has arrived.*

Kraev tapped on the screen of his wristband, and a cool voice spoke in his ear.

*"Kraev ek-Tayn, a genetic match has been found for you. The details on your match are the following. Name: Olivia Griffin. Species: human. Planet of origin: Earth..."*

Kraev almost dropped his fruit.

Zevyk frowned at him. "Kraev, what's wrong?"

*"...Your match will arrive at your current location on R-2841 within the next hour,"* the message continued. *"Congratulations."*

A huge grin broke out on Kraev's face. "Nothing is wrong," he said. "In fact, everything is *very* right." He turned to Zevyk, his entire body buzzing with excitement. "A match has been found for me!"

Zevyk's eyes widened momentarily before he grinned right back. "The fates have favored you this day." He clapped Kraev on the back. "Congratulations, brother."

He and Zevyk weren't actually siblings, but they were as close as it got without being blood-related. When Zevyk's family had been killed in the war nearly twenty-five years ago, Kraev's family had taken him in and the two of them had grown up together.

"The message said she is a human from planet Earth." Kraev frowned. Not that her species really mattered, but... "I've never seen a human before. Have you?"

Zevyk shook his head. "I don't think there are humans on R-2841. I'm not even sure there are any on Raewan. Isn't Earth the newest planet the Mahdfel have made an agreement with?"

"Maybe…" Kraev's voice faltered, but it wasn't nerves or doubt in his voice. He could hardly stay still with how excited he was. "I can't remember news of humans going to Raewan."

"It's a long time since we've been home."

The longing to see his family again tugged at Kraev. It had been a long time. Two years, maybe even more. But as soon as the melancholy hit him, it disappeared, replaced by joy.

"I can't wait to have a big family of my own." He was the oldest of six brothers, and he wanted just as many children. "A family of strong warriors to carry on our traditions." He grinned. "I can't wait to meet her."

Zevyk gave him a short, one-armed hug. "I'm happy for you, my brother."

Kraev was hit by a sudden wave of nerves. He hadn't expected a match, not right now. Of course, he had always hoped for one, but… Had he tidied his quarters well enough? What about the gift he'd had for years, sitting ready and waiting to give to his mate when she was found? Was it good enough?

It was a Raewani tradition that a male gave his mate a gift to demonstrate his commitment and ability to care for her. Had he gotten enough demonstrate that to his human female? He looked at the fruit in his hand. Maybe he could collect some to take to her as well. She would most likely have never had anything like this before on her home planet.

His wristband flashed again and he expected it to be an alert that his mate was being teleported. His nerves vanished and then returned in full force when he noticed the color of the message. This time, the light was orange. His whole body stiffened in horror. From the corner of his eye, he could see that Zevyk's wristband was flashing too.

*In alarm.*

Despite Kraev's earlier words that the Suhlik probably wouldn't dare to attack anytime soon after their failure last night, it seemed that the lizards had not only attacked the planet again… They had breached its defenses.

This was the worst possible timing. His mate would be coming here now, and she would be walking right into the middle of a deadly attack if the Suhlik managed to land.

"I have to go," he said, fighting back the rising panic. He'd never panicked in the face of a Suhlik attack before. He was a warrior. All Mahdfel went through vigorous warrior training from birth. He had been trained for this his entire life. He'd never been afraid of the Suhlik before.

But now, he was terrified. The first place the Suhlik would try to take control of on R-2841 was the planet's most tactical location: the teleport base. The very teleport base where his match was currently being teleported.

A hard lump stuck in Kraev's throat and his stomach felt suddenly empty despite the fruit he had just eaten. He might lose his mate the moment he got her. He might not even get to see her alive.

"Go, Kraev," Zevyk said, bringing him back from his panicked thoughts. "You need to get to the teleport base. I'll report to the Warlord that you have been matched and that you have gone after your mate. It will be fine."

"Yes." Kraev rose immediately to action. It would be fine. It had to be.

He started on a fast-paced run out of the greenhouse and toward the entrance of the volcano where the fighter ships were kept. He was a pilot. He could do this. He could push the ship as quickly as possible toward the teleport base, where his mate would be waiting.

He would get to her before the Suhlik did.

He allowed himself a single glimpse at the sky and saw that it was full of Suhlik ships, and the Mahdfel ones flying fast to meet them.

With his heart in his throat, he quickened his pace.

He wasn't going to let anything happen to his mate.

# 3

## OLIVIA

OLIVIA GASPED FOR AIR.

She felt like she hadn't been breathing for minutes. Her head spun and she stumbled on her feet, her legs threatening to give in. Leaning onto the metallic frame of the teleporter, she tried to balance herself. Her heart pounded in her chest and her breath came out in short pants.

When she had entered the teleporter, a bright white light had swallowed her, penetrating through her eyelids and blinding her completely. Everything around her had disappeared and she hadn't been able to see or hear anything, like she had been sucked into some sort of a vacuum – which probably a very accurate description of what had happened.

Now, her senses were slowly returning to her.

She dug the mint out of her pocket, stuffed it into her mouth, and sucked hard. The cool flavor of the candy decreased the spinning in her head just a little, but she still felt like sitting in front of a toilet until the nausea passed. She hoped it *would* pass.

After closing her eyes for a second and getting used to the sicky feeling, she realized that no one was in the room with her. There wasn't someone waiting to greet her or lead her away to her alien husband. Even to just explain to her what was going to happen next. There was no one else in the room at all.

Olivia stepped out of the teleporter. The room itself was quite small, with only one entrance on the other side. The teleporter took up the vast majority of the space and blocked her view from the rest of the metal room.

Orange lights were flashing. Strangely, it gave the cold metal interior an almost warm feel. But orange didn't seem like a reassuring color for flashing lights. Was it some kind of alert? Was that why there wasn't anyone here to greet her?

She turned back to the machine and looked at the control pad on the side. This was what the soldier on Earth had used to send her here. Maybe she could use it to send herself back. If no one was here to receive her anyway, couldn't she just leave?

None of the buttons were labeled, though. Olivia turned back to the room and waited. Surely, someone would come pick her up. Weren't the Mahdfel desperate for females?

But when the minutes ticked by and no one came, Olivia started to worry. The room was eerily quiet and the silence made her feel uneasy. Somewhere deep inside, she sensed that this wasn't normal. This wasn't how it was supposed to be here.

Gathering up her courage, she called out, "Hello?"

Her voice echoed slightly. That's how dead quiet it was around her. She waited again, for someone to answer her or for anything at all, but only silence surrounded her.

When no one answered her for another minute, Olivia stepped back into the teleporter, hitting on some buttons and hoping for a miracle. Hoping that it would suck her back in and throw her back to where she came from. She could explain that it was a mistake, that she'd gone but there was no one there. It obviously wasn't meant to be.

Then, out of the corner of her eye, she spotted something. A crumpled light blue figure sprawled across the floor, behind a desk. The alien's head was shaved except for a series of thick braids running across his skull in lines. Two large horns protruded from his head and a smaller third one from just above his forehead. Turquoise eyes stared unseeingly into the room.

Olivia gasped. She wanted to scream, but the sound got stuck in her throat. Blood pooled underneath the alien from a large wound in his stomach, exposed by a gaping tear in the embroidered fabric of the top he was wearing.

The scream finally came when another alien appeared in the open doorway of the room.

Unnaturally tall, it had golden scales and eyes with a reptilian slit that stared straight at her. The retractable claws in the alien's hands and elbows extended as he glared at her. Inches long, they were sharp as knives.

The Suhlik looked exactly as she remembered them. Beautiful. Eerie. Creepy. *Dangerous.*

She took a singular step away, her back hitting the end of the teleporter. The alien's thin lips spread into a humorless smile, revealing rows and rows of sharp teeth.

Crap. So this was how she died. A few minutes onto a planet halfway across the universe and she'd stepped straight into the path of a Suhlik warrior for the first time since they'd first invaded Earth. Hadn't the nurse said she wouldn't be sent anywhere unsafe? Because this seemed pretty damn unsafe.

She almost wanted to laugh. This was just her luck. Be matched to an alien and then ripped to shreds by another.

She looked at the Suhlik directly in the eye. He was lean and muscular – and probably faster than a cheetah. If she waited for him to act, he would have her pinned down in a split second.

She didn't wait.

She hopped out of the teleporter and jumped to the side. The Suhlik leaped after her, but in doing so, he moved away from the door. Taking her chances, Olivia charged as fast as she could away from the lizard and toward the now-clear opening.

She dashed into the corridor, pure adrenaline fueling her legs and completely removing the nausea that had moments before been almost crippling. She could hear the Suhlik start to run behind her. The orange lights flashed in the corridor around them and now, she could hear the sounds of fighting somewhere in the distance too.

Olivia had never been an athlete, but now, she ran faster than she ever had in her life.

It wasn't enough.

It wasn't long before the Suhlik caught her with

his long legs. The lizard had always been going to catch her.

He threw her against the wall with one clean sweep of his arm. She twisted on her ankle as she fell and slammed her head against the metal wall. The Suhlik dragged her straight back up again and shoved her, knocking the back of her head against the wall this time. She groaned, pain shooting through her skull and fear making her heart thud against her rib cage.

With all her strength, Olivia struggled desperately in the vicious alien's grip as the male hissed and almost seemed to leer at her. She knew she was dead, but instincts demanded that she keep fighting. She wasn't going to just give in.

Then, suddenly, the lizard's grip on her loosened. She slumped and, for a second, she thought he was going to collapse onto her and crush her completely. But something intervened, pulling the monster away and flinging its corpse to the side.

It wasn't until the Suhlik hit the ground – she couldn't keep looking at the horrifyingly beautiful golden face – that Olivia saw the round hole through the side of his head.

Her eyes flicked back. Looking ahead, she saw the man who had saved her.

A huge, muscular, bright blue alien stood in front

of her with a chiseled but worried face. His eyes were clear turquoise and his head was shaved except for a mass of braids that ran down the center and down his back. Two longer horns protruded from the side of his head, and a smaller one poked through the middle of the braid. A long tail swished behind his back. He wore a colorful embroidered tunic that looked like some kind of light armor, and she could see a mass of swirling tattoos on the hardened muscle of his blue arms.

Looking at him was the strangest experience.

Olivia had never been face-to-face with a *friendly* alien before. When the Mahdfel had come and liberated Earth, she had been hiding away from them. Her father had insisted that they not interact with them, as if she would have ever gone and attempted to be friends with an alien power, even if they had just given Earth their freedom back.

But this man had just saved her life. Now, he was standing opposite her, staring at her with his pupil-less, turquoise eyes, and she didn't know whether to be terrified or grateful.

She chose grateful for the moment. "Thank you."

Part of her didn't expect the translator in her ear to actually work, but the man nodded, his eyes still fixed on her. "My mate?" he asked. He reached out as if to touch her, and she flinched away automatically. He dropped his hand immediately.

"You... you're *Crave*?" she asked, skeptical. She couldn't remember if that had actually been his name. The half an hour or so since hearing the words "you're a match" had been such a blur, made only worse by the teleportation that had messed with her head. But the alien smiled.

"Kra-ev. Kraev," he corrected, his voice so deep her stomach fluttered. She'd never thought an alien would elicit such a response in her. "And you are my mate." He breathed deeply as if her smell had any relevance to that statement. "Owl-ee-vee-a."

He pronounced her name so carefully and slowly – and so utterly wrong that Olivia couldn't help but smile despite everything. She immediately felt better about getting his name wrong. "Olivia," she said. "Short i's."

The alien nodded at her with a smile, his tail swaying gently behind him. But then his whole body tensed and his expression grew serious. He turned in the corridor, as if he'd heard something.

"Olivia, we need to leave here." His voice was a notch harder and cold.

The reality of the situation kicked in immediately and Olivia's heart leaped in her chest. She looked down at the corpse of the Suhlik and fought the tremors running through her body. Kraev hesitated and then gave her hand a quick squeeze.

"Quickly," he urged. "Before more come. I need to protect you."

She breathed deeply, trying to sort out the mess in her mind, and then nodded. It made her head ache.

"Yeah. Okay. Let's go."

# 4

## KRAEV

HIS MATE WAS BEAUTIFUL.

The moment Kraev laid eyes upon her, he was drawn to her. The tattoos on his skin tingled at her nearness and his tail swayed with urgency to touch her. Despite everything that was happening, all he could think about was how gorgeous his mate was.

Olivia. The name sounded strange on his tongue, but he liked it. She looked unlike anything he had ever seen in his life. She had pale skin and shoulder-length hair the color of sunshine. She was so small and fragile that his heart had nearly burst when he'd seen her being thrown about by the Suhlik.

The lizard had not died fast enough.

Olivia's scent floated in the air around them. Like *amihae* fruit and a spice he couldn't quite name. It was the sweetest scent he'd ever smelled in his life, pure perfection. He wanted to bury his face in her hair and inhale deeply. He wanted to wrap her in his arms and carry her back to his bed right then and there.

But first, they needed to get out of the teleport base.

"We need to head for my ship," he said, turning in the direction they needed to go, but looking over his shoulder to make sure that Olivia was right there beside him.

Suhlik had infiltrated the whole teleport base, and although his fellow Mahdfel were doing their best to keep them occupied, they would be in danger as long as they stayed there.

"What's going on?" Olivia asked, following him down the hallway. His mate was obviously terrified, her brown eyes wide and her hands shaking at her sides. "I thought this was supposed to be a safe planet. They're only supposed to send brides to safe locations."

"You'll always be safe with me," Kraev responded, even though he knew he couldn't guarantee it. Suhlik attacks on the planet were clearly getting worse. The lizards hadn't managed to get on the surface for years. And now they had.

Maybe she shouldn't have been sent here. She was so small and it had already been proven that humans weren't good matches for fighting against the Suhlik. Maybe sending her to this planet had been a bad idea.

But she was here beside him and his tattoos were pulsing in unison with his heart at the knowledge that he'd found his mate. He'd found the woman who was going to give him the family he'd always dreamed of. He would never regret that.

He noticed she was limping slightly as they walked deeper into the hallway, and he came to an immediate stop. "Is your leg okay?"

"It's fine, just keep going," she urged.

Kraev frowned. "No, you're hurt."

Her face was strained, betraying the pain, but she shook her head. Even that made her grimace. "You said it yourself, we need to get out of here. My ankle is just a little sprained. It's not a big deal. Please."

"I can't–"

She rested a small hand on his bare forearm. "*Please*. Before more Suhlik come."

It went against everything he knew to let his mate hobble along beside him without helping, but she was right. They needed to get out of there before more of the damned lizards came, and he needed his hands on his weapon in case they *did* show up.

Just as the thought appeared in his mind, a door

at the end of the corridor opened and three Suhlik walked in.

Kraev pushed Olivia back into the hallway they had come from, but it was too late.

They had been spotted.

He'd have to fight.

One Suhlik was a strong warrior, but three Suhlik was a lot for one man. Kraev wished that Zevyk was by his side. Despite having specialized in engineering, Zevyk had undergone the same warrior training he had. Together, they could have taken the bastards down in no time.

As it was, he was alone. His tail swatted with anxiety, but he knew he couldn't fail now. He refused to fail his newfound mate.

Quickly, he pulled a smaller gun from his hip and pressed it to Olivia's hand.

"Use it if you need to," he said, hoping she knew how to actually fire the weapon.

He would fight with everything in him to make sure that he survived to keep his mate safe and to get to know her, but sometimes willpower alone wasn't enough to get someone through a battle. His father's death had taught him that.

He'd expected his mate to protest, but instead, she nodded and stood beside him.

"No, stand back," he said. "Far behind me. You'll be safe around the corner."

This time, she did hesitate, looking up at him. His gaze burned back into hers, and although Kraev could see fear glittering in her brown eyes, he could also see determination. The fates really had favored him.

She finally nodded and stood back. The footsteps of the Suhlik guards approached in the other hallway, and Kraev launched himself around the corner. He aimed his gun at the approaching Suhlik and fired off toward the trio.

The stream of shots caught one of the lizards in the head, taking him down immediately. That left him two on one. He could cope with that.

Unfortunately, the two other guards weren't about to make the same mistake as their friend. Kraev ducked to the side when one of the Suhlik shot at him. He aimed at the lizard but missed by an arm's length when the male moved. The other guard rushed straight toward him and Kraev jumped to avoid his shot, but not before the first one aimed again.

There was nowhere to hide.

Kraev shielded himself with his gun. The shots missed him just barely, but they blasted into the weapon's core.

Dammit. He grimaced, throwing the now-useless gun away. He glared at the Suhlik, pulling knives from his belt. The poison-infused blades were designed specifically to get beneath the armored scales of a Suhlik's body, and straight into flesh.

He dashed toward the lizards, ducking and jumping to avoid their shots. He quickly got close enough to make their guns useless in the close-combat fight, but the lizards still had an advantage against him: their claws.

Kraev was strong in hand-to-hand combat, but it wasn't his specialty. He was a pilot, and he felt much more comfortable forcing Suhlik ships from the sky than he did engaging them in close quarters like this.

The Suhlik who had breached the base, however, were specialists in hand-to-hand. Kraev was already at a disadvantage, but he didn't let it stop him. As a Mahdfel, he had increased strength and speed. He would use them to outwit the brazen Suhlik who thought they could hurt his mate.

He parried vicious attacks from the Suhlik claws and fought back with slashing attacks, but the lizards were just as quick. He curved his back away from the claws on their elbows as they went in together for a simultaneous attack, and then dashed back in, quicker than they could have done themselves.

A knife pierced the left-hand side of one's stomach, but it wasn't a wound that would kill him. Kraev continued to get hits, but none of them were fatal, and soon, he started taking hits himself. One of their elbow blades sliced across his chest. It wasn't deep, but it easily could have been. A close call gave him a graze on his neck.

Knowing his mate was behind him threatened to distract him. He wanted to tell her to run, but there was nowhere to go. She couldn't fit past their fight to make it to the hangar and back the way they'd come would only lead her deeper into the building.

It was up to him to lead her out. He could not afford to lose this fight.

Kraev dodged backward, barely moving out of the way of a slice that would have cut straight across his eye. Then, out of nowhere, a shot echoed in the hallway and one of the Suhlik fell to the ground, a hole in his head much like the ones Kraev had put through two Suhlik so far today.

He briefly glanced over his shoulder. Olivia was holding the gun he had given her in her hand, aimed at where the lizard's head had been just seconds ago. Her arm was steady and her face was flat. Almost immediately, her hand started to tremor again.

Impressed and worried, Kraev wanted to go and wrap her in his arms, but he still had one lizard to take down. There was no doubt that he'd be the victor in the fight now. One-on-one, the Suhlik had no chance.

Kraev smiled viciously at the lizard. He dodged frenzied attacks from the Suhlik that knew he was about to die, and then darted forward and pierced the male's neck with his two blades, pushing him down to the floor as he did. When he pulled them back, they were covered in the grimy blood of the lizard.

He turned immediately back to Olivia, who was holding the gun limply at her side and staring at the Suhlik she'd killed.

"I never thought I'd be able to get my revenge on one of them," she whispered quietly. It was clear that killing a living being – even if it was a Suhlik – had gotten to her, and Kraev wanted to comfort her. His tail twitched with a need to wrap around her, but he refrained, knowing how she'd reacted when he'd touched her earlier.

"You did great," he said. "Where did you learn to fight like that?"

Olivia shook her head. "I can't fight. Not at all. But I'm a decent shot. My family went into hiding for a long time after the Suhlik invasion. My dad taught me to shoot." She held the gun back out to him. "Here."

Kraev stopped her and picked up one of the Suhlik's guns from the floor. "You keep it," he said. "I'd feel better if you were armed."

She hesitated but then nodded. "Okay." She took a couple of steps closer to him and seemed to relax a little when she was beside him.

"Let's keep moving," he said. He just wanted this to be over so that he could be somewhere safe with his mate. There was so much he wanted to know. So much he wanted to say. This wasn't at all how it had been supposed to go and he wanted to make up for that.

"What's really going on here?" Olivia asked as they moved quickly down the corridors. The tremor in her voice had calmed down a little and it soothed him too. "Is this just really bad timing, or does this kind of thing happen often?"

"A bit of both," he replied. "Suhlik attacks on R-2841 are rather frequent, but this is also a really bad timing. The lizards haven't actually made it to the surface of the planet for years until today."

"Why? Why do they want this planet?"

"R-2841 is abundant with an incredibly rare and powerful mineral called hellstone. It prevents teleportation and is crucial for the defense of any location. The Suhlik also use it for their experiments." His tail lashed angrily at the thought.

"That's why they're here. They want to control the planet and get the hellstone. It could be a powerful weapon if it was used by them."

He glanced to the side and saw Olivia visibly shudder. "So they'll keep coming back, even if they fail this time."

His throat was dry. "Yes. They'll keep coming back."

He slowed and put a hand out to stop Olivia and bring her in close to the wall. "Around the corner is the hangar," he said. "Through a pair of double doors. It might be swarming with Suhlik. This could be dangerous, but it's a better idea than hiding. They travel in groups and if they find us, they might kill us. We need to get as far away from here as possible."

"Why aren't you with people?" she asked. "Don't you travel in groups to try and counter that?"

"Normally, yes. The Mahdfel defending the planet are all in groups. But I came here by myself to make sure you were okay."

"You risked your life for me?" She looked up at him with big eyes.

He blinked. "Of course. You're my mate." He would do the same again every time without a second's hesitation.

She opened her mouth and then shut it again. "Oh," she said softly.

Kraev brought his wristband to his mouth and said quietly, "Zevyk."

The wristband immediately opened a channel with his best friend.

"Kraev," came the quick, but stressed-sounding, response. "I'm so glad to hear from you, brother. What can I do for you?"

"Can you get eyes on the hangar at the teleport base?" Zevyk was an engineer and, as such, his main role right now would be onboard one of the fighting ships in the sky above, doing his best to repair any damage done. He might have access to camera feeds.

"One moment," Zevyk said, the words drawn out. "Yes. Got it. There's a firefight going on in the hangar. Which door are you behind?"

He gave his friend their location.

"There's a path for you to a ship, but it's risky. Is it just you, or did you find your mate?"

"She's with me."

"I'm glad." Zevyk sounded just as relieved as Kraev felt. "When you exit the door, you need to go right and skirt the wall until you get to a ship. You should be able to get there without being noticed, but it's a mess in there, Kraev. Hand-to-hand and guns. Ships are taking off and landing all the time. It's risky."

"Not as risky as staying in the base. I have no idea

who might find us then. We need to get out of here. I need to keep Olivia safe."

"I know," Zevyk replied. There was suddenly static on the line. "My ship is hit. I've got to go. Good luck, my brother."

"And you, brother."

Kraev allowed himself just a moment of worry for Zevyk before returning to the task at hand. "Did you hear all that?" he asked Olivia.

She nodded. "Yes. I've got it."

"Are you okay to run on your ankle?"

"I'll be fine. It's not that bad, I promise."

He dithered for a second. The need to carry her and ensure she was well nearly overwhelmed him. But carrying her while he needed his hands free to shoot was not only unrealistic, it was stupid.

"Okay," he finally said.

He wanted to wrap her in his arms and kiss her senseless just in case this was the only opportunity he was going to have for it. His tail swayed in anticipation and his tattoos tingled on his skin. She looked up at him with these big, nervous but somehow trusting eyes and he knew he was going to be the happiest man in the world if they made it out alive.

"I'm glad you're here," he said instead.

Olivia laughed, which wasn't the reaction he'd expected. "I'm not sure I can say the same."

The weight of disappointment settled on his stomach. He guessed he couldn't blame her. Being sent to an active battle zone must have come as a shock. But still, did she not feel the same as him? Did she not have that sense that they were absolutely meant for each other? He had always thought that when the time came and he was matched, he would immediately have a bond with his mate, like his parents did.

Doubt filtered into his heart. He knew that humans were different, that their culture was different, but he was already so certain that they were perfect together. Did she not feel it? The genetic matching did not lie.

She must have seen his doubts on his face because she rested a hand on his forearm again. The contact made his tattoos glow softly as the desire to pull her into his arms ratcheted up.

"I'm glad I've met you," she said gently. "Without you, I'd already be toast. And, well, this is probably the most excitement I've ever had in my life, I guess."

Her words were encouraging, but there was something bitter in that statement. He was sure she was lying about the excitement, maybe even about meeting him. The idea felt uneasy in his mind, but he shoved it aside. He'd ask her about it later. Right now, they needed to move.

"Let's go."

He squeezed her hand and then guided her to the double doors. They were solid metal and soundproofed. There was no way to know what they were walking into until it was too late. He half expected the doors to open and Suhlik to come charging over them.

He keyed in the code that would allow them to pass and held the Suhlik weapon tightly in his grip, ready to shoot anything that came at him.

Inside the hangar was chaos. The configuration of the fight seemed to have changed even since Zevyk had been looking at the screen. Now, the Mahdfel were guarding the door that Kraev and Olivia walked through, clearly trying to prevent the Suhlik from getting through to where the teleporter was.

It meant that they walked straight into the middle of the hottest area in the hangar. Kraev wrapped his arm around Olivia's head to shield it from any stray bullets before dragging her right like Zevyk had instructed. He shot toward the Suhlik but focused on moving as quickly as possible. Olivia was practically skipping beside him, trying to move as quickly with her damaged ankle.

Shame shot through him. He should never have been making her do something that caused her pain. He wasn't being a good mate.

The rest of the Mahdfel defending the door kept their backs and he shouted a few words to them to tell them what he was doing. In return, they promised to keep the fighting as far from Kraev and Olivia as possible. They all understood his actions. No one tried to tell him it was his duty to stand and fight with the rest of them.

Family always came first.

They made it out of the main fighting with Kraev only receiving a couple of grazes to his arms. They would heal in no time. He wanted to stop to make sure Olivia hadn't been hurt, but there wasn't time. They moved around the side of the Mahdfel ship he was intending to use and found two Suhlik striding toward him.

Both Olivia and Kraev shot at the same time. Luckily, they picked a different one each, and the Suhlik fell to the ground, neither even getting a chance to start their charge. Olivia's shot hadn't quite killed the lizard, hitting the male in the shoulder, but Kraev easily finished him off.

It was almost easy to fall into the trap of thinking of Olivia as another warrior when she acted so quickly and accurately like that. But then they reached the door to the ship and he caught a glance of her. She was pale except for two spots of red on her cheeks. She was panting rather than breathing and kept glancing back at the Suhlik they'd just killed.

She wasn't a warrior. She was just a scared human who'd been put in a nightmarish situation and was trying to do her best in it.

"Here," he said, wanting to keep talking to her to distract her from the dead lizards. "I'm just going to open the door to this ship and then we'll be out of here." He put his thumb on a panel on the side of the small fighter ship as he said it, and the door clicked open, recognizing his credentials.

"Come on," he took her hand and gave her a boost into the small ship. It wasn't big enough to spend more than a few hours on. There was no bathroom, no beds. It was purely for close quarters, high-paced fighting, and that was exactly what he needed right now. Something fast and agile to get as far away from the Suhlik as possible.

And he would get Olivia away from the Suhlik, no matter what.

He would get her out and he would win her heart. This, he promised to himself.

# 5

## OLIVIA

OLIVIA'S HEART pounded in her chest. She thought she might have a heart attack as Kraev guided her to one of the two seats inside the tiny ship that he'd selected. It looked small compared to most of the others in the hangar.

"Is this really the ship we want?" she asked, panic threatening to overwhelm her senses. "It's so small. Is it safe?"

She sat back into the chair, trying to take deep breaths. She could hear the fighting in the hangar still, see the bodies of the Suhlik they'd killed. The ones *she'd* killed. She didn't regret it, but it had hit her a little harder than she expected it to, and she struggled to stay focused on the now.

"This one is faster," Kraev replied, strapping her into the seat.

His fingers brushed against her skin through the thin blouse she was wearing and she was ashamed to say that it sent a thrill through her. It was probably just the adrenaline talking. Just too much excitement in one day, even if she'd been sarcastic when she'd said that to him earlier.

He might be gorgeous in a brutish, exotic kind of way, but she wasn't ready to admit that she might like the idea of him touching her properly, beyond the few bits of light contact they'd had so far. She'd heard some Mahdfel brides practically fell on their backs when they met their matches, but Olivia wasn't that kind of a girl. She preferred to know her partner first.

Besides, she might not even make it through all this alive to face the consequences of those thoughts anyway.

"The Suhlik ships will be bigger since they've traveled through space to get here. We should be able to outmaneuver them in a smaller ship. The bigger ships would also require at least two pilots or a full crew. Since it's just me, I need to be able to navigate, fire weapons, and fly all at once."

Guilt settled in her stomach. She was weighing him down.

"Is there anything I can do?"

He seemed to consider her words as he strapped himself into the pilot's seat beside her.

"You can help me watch out for Suhlik ships," he finally said, but Olivia couldn't help but think he'd given her a useless task just to stay focused. At least on the ground, she'd been able to do something, react somehow. Run, duck, or even shoot, despite how surprised she had been by that fact.

But in the air, she could do nothing but sit back and hope for the best.

Kraev reorganized some of the screens around him and then flicked a few switches on the dashboard, preparing for take-off.

Olivia glanced out of the windows of the ship. She saw the Mahdfel and Suhlik still fighting in the hangar. The Suhlik paid them no attention in the ship, but Olivia feared their fight was only about to begin once they took off and joined whatever ships were out there. Somewhere in the distance, an explosion went off, shaking the ground.

"It might be a bumpy ride," Kraev said as the engines started. The ship vibrated slightly under their power and Olivia gripped the sides of her seat. "I'm not sure how fast I'll be able to go. Your body won't be able to take as much G-force as mine and I don't want to risk hurting you."

"Do whatever you need to do," she said, her heart

thumping anxiously in her chest. She had been on an airplane a few times as a child, but this was something entirely different, even if you didn't account for the fact that they were in a war zone. "Don't even think about the fact I'm here."

"I'm always going to be thinking about you, Olivia," Kraev said. His words should have been cheesy, but his expression told her he was being completely sincere. She didn't know what to make out of that. A strange wave of warmth spread through her toward the alien who was risking his life to try and keep her alive.

The ship began to move, slowly at first, but when it took off in the air, Olivia's heart leaped. Her knuckles turned white as she gripped her seat, waiting for the G-force to shove her back. It came quickly and she sucked in a gasp as it felt like someone sat on her chest. Within seconds, they flew out of the hangar and into the sky above the planet.

In any other situation, it would have been thrilling. She would have been grinning and laughing as she experienced something completely different from normal. A spaceship on a planet halfway across the universe? It was madness. It was surreal, even though she'd known about the existence of aliens since she was a child.

Instead, all she could feel was dread.

Looking out of the window in front of her, she could see the sky full of ships. Red and orange trails and smoke filled the sky between them all. Some of them were performing high-speed maneuvers and some appeared to be completely still in the air. She had no idea how many people were out there and how many would have already lost their lives.

When Kraev shouted, "We've got two on our tail," over the sound of the engines, the thundering of her heart didn't calm down at all.

"What are we going to do?" Her voice sounded panicked even to her own ears, and as she glanced behind them, she saw the two Suhlik ships Kraev was talking about.

"I've got the weapons systems on autopilot. They should be able to deal with any incoming missiles."

Olivia sat back and closed her eyes, imagining the ship being blown to smithereens. It was hard to breathe at the speed they were traveling at and the panic wasn't making things any easier.

This was supposed to be safe.

She was supposed to have come to a peaceful planet to make a thousand babies for her new husband, not to almost be killed and end up in a high-speed spaceship chase against the Suhlik.

Admittedly, as she opened her eyes and looked out of the window in front of her, she wasn't sure the alternative was much better. Either way, she lost her life as she knew it.

"Incoming missiles," Kraev shouted. "I've got to barrel roll, hold on tight."

Olivia swallowed a scream as the ship did a full roll in the sky, making the straps holding her in place strain against her weight. Then they were back to being the right way up and she could almost breathe again.

"They're gaining on us," he said. "I can't go any faster. I might injure you."

"I'll be okay," she promised. "Do what you have to do." There was no way she was going to be responsible for this man's death after he'd already risked so much. Her getting a little bit hurt was preferable to them both ending up in a fiery tangle on the ground.

"Okay," he said, though it was through gritted teeth and she knew he didn't want to. He kept talking to her as the pressure on her chest increased and breathing became even more difficult. She wasn't going to try and force words out unless she absolutely had to.

Him speaking worked, though. It was calming to hear his soothing voice as the calamity raged in the sky around them.

"I'm heading for the mountains. There's nothing

of strategic value out there. No reason that the Suhlik should chase us except to kill. Though obviously, you know that they kill for the fun of it. But hopefully, it'll give us some coverage. We might be able to hide there until the fighting is– Shit."

Before Olivia could take notice of whatever had made him curse, the ship shot up to the skies. Pressure loaded even further on top of Olivia and she really did stop breathing for a moment.

Then, it returned to normal and she gasped.

An explosion hit the nearby mountain in the location they had been. Olivia sucked in a breath. The ship did another flip as Kraev pulled back the controls, and they barely avoided yet another missile.

"Stars," Kraev breathed. "They seem intent on following us. I need to do something." He rapidly tapped the screen in front of him.

"What are you doing?" Olivia managed to gasp out. The words came out choked and her head spun from all the twirling they had done, but the absence of his calm, explanatory voice was enough to let the terror force its way back in.

"I'm going to launch a manual attack against the ships. The switch-up of tactics from computer to manual might do the trick. It might– Yes!" His voice was full of emotion and it made her heart swell.

From the corner of her eye, Olivia saw a large explosion in the air as a Suhlik ship fell toward the ground.

"Got the bastard," he said. "One down, one to go. But dammit, missiles incoming, brace yourself."

This ship swerved up and down and to the left again, but as they reached the mountain range, the space to avoid the missiles diminished. Kraev pulled the controls and turned the ship to the right, straight in the direction of a large mountain.

Olivia gasped, but he quickly twirled the ship again, away from the rapidly approaching wall of rock. The wings of the ship nearly scraped the mountain, but the missile flew behind them, hitting the stone wall. Boulders from the explosion fell in their direction and some of the smaller rocks hit the roof of the ship. Another missile was already on its way, and this time, Kraev's quick maneuvering wasn't enough to stop it from making contact.

The missile struck in the side of the ship, and suddenly, they were spinning worse than before. The whole ship shook from the power of the impact and Olivia was thrust forward in her seat.

"Dammit," Kraev hissed, rapidly pressing buttons on his dashboard. "The left engine is hit. We're going down!"

Olivia's heart jumped at his words. They had

stopped spinning and had gone straight down to falling. From the corner of her eye, Olivia could see flames as the ship – and the engine – burned. Stars, it wasn't going to explode, was it?

Kraev gripped the controls, clearly still trying to ease their landing as much as possible, but the mountains were approaching fast.

"Are we... Are we going to die?"

The words tumbled out of her mouth, but all she could feel was disbelief. This couldn't be happening. She couldn't die.

"Not if I can help it," Kraev gritted through his teeth. "Hold on tight!"

In that moment, facing near-certain death, all Olivia could think about was her family and the life she would never have. She was distracted just for a second by how beautiful everything looked around them. Mountains rose high into the sky, past the cloud line. Snow covered them, even in the foothills. It looked freezing out there. Deadly, but stunning.

It was the last thing she saw before darkness swallowed her.

# 6

## KRAEV

KRAEV WOKE up with a pounding head and more pains that slowly revealed themselves as he came further into consciousness. His ears rung and a sharp pain throbbed on his side. He groaned at the pain, trying to remember what had happened.

The memories came back to him in flashes. Finding out about his mate, the Suhlik attack, the chase...

"Olivia," he breathed, his voice oddly hoarse as if he hadn't had a drop of water for days.

He urgently looked around, but could not see her anywhere. He was outside, lying on a gradual hill somewhere in the mountains. Clearly, the evacuation protocol of the ship had kicked in at last minute and launched them out, still tied to their seats and parachutes.

Or at least… It had launched *him* out.

Dread filled him at the thought and he scrambled up from his seat. His muscles burned with every movement and blood dripped to the ground from a wound in his chest, but he didn't care. Nothing would hurt more than the pain of losing his mate when he'd only just found her.

He dragged himself to his feet, frantically looking around for Olivia.

He didn't have to look far. In his panic, he'd missed the fact that she was lying just a few feet behind him, sprawled across the ground.

His heart immediately sank at the sight. He hurried over to her, ignoring the searing pain in his side and chest. She looked paler than before, but aside for a few scrapes, she didn't seem injured on the outside. Still, her unmoving form filled him with alarm.

*Please, simply be unconscious…*

He rolled her over to her side and pressed a finger to her neck, checking for a pulse. A slow but steady rhythm told him that she'd survived the crash too, and a heavy breath escaped his lungs. The relief that swelled in his chest was so overwhelming that he almost just lay down beside her to get himself back together.

*Thank the stars.*

Kraev turned to look at the sky, wondering how long they had been unconscious. It was still bright outside, and the moons were not yet visible, so it must not have been more than an hour or two. He could still see the fight in full swing in the direction of the teleport base and it seemed like it was starting to move further afield too.

They would have to move, and quickly, or else a stray Suhlik ship might catch sight of them and decide to end them for good.

"Zevyk." He tried to use his wristband to contact his friend, and when that didn't work, he tried the main base.

Nothing.

The screen of his band worked, but it didn't seem to be able to send or receive signals anymore. Dammit. It must have broken in the crash, and he didn't have the knowledge to repair it.

It looked like they were going to be stuck in the mountains for a couple of days then.

Seeing no other choice, Kraev carefully lifted Olivia from the ground, pulling her into his arms. He cradled her body against his chest, not caring that it was aggravating his wounds. They would heal quickly, even if not immediately. He knew they weren't life-threatening, but staying out in the open while the fight was ongoing was.

A short distance away, he could see the crashed spaceship. Landing in a thick snowdrift meant that it hadn't burst into flames, but it was completely destroyed in all the ways that mattered. The engine was dead and the shell full of holes, mangled and distorted. The windows were shattered and the whole left side of it was torn where it had clearly scraped a mountain. It was nothing more than scrap metal now.

But inside it were plenty of things that he would need if they were going to be stuck in the mountains.

He walked slowly toward the ship with Olivia in his arms. At the ship, he set her down on a wing so that she wouldn't be left to shiver in the cold. His mate clearly couldn't take the cold weather well. She was already freezing to the touch, and that was worrying him. He hurried inside the spaceship to gather supplies as quickly as possible.

He grabbed the first-aid kit, the rations and clean water that were always stored within Mahdfel spaceships on the planet, and picked an extra parachute from the back of the ship. It wasn't overly thick material and was huge, but it would be something that he could wrap Olivia in to try to warm her up.

Then, he exited the ship and went back to Olivia,

hoisting her once more into his arms, bridal style, even though it made it harder to carry the supplies he'd retrieved. But there was no way he was going to throw her over his shoulder like a piece of meat, especially when she was injured. He might cause more damage than good.

The progress across the mountainside wasn't fast, and he was on high alert, both looking for caves that he could shelter in and making sure that no ships were passing too close overhead.

When he came across a cave, it wasn't a large one, but it was plenty big enough to keep them both out of sight and sheltered from the elements until she woke up and he could see how injured she actually was. Smaller was sometimes better, anyway. It meant there wasn't likely to be any wildlife in it.

Not that there was much wildlife on R-2841 in the first place. It was a desolate planet, with barely any animals or plants. The Mahdfel had come across it by chance on a cataloging mission. They had only realized just how valuable it was as a strategic resource after hellstone had been discovered in the volcanoes.

Inside the cave, he did his best to make Olivia as comfortable as possible, wrapping her in the parachute and then going to collect whatever he could find to build a fire. He was skeptical of setting a fire that might attract attention with the smoke, but he was more terrified by the thought of his mate freezing to death. Mahdfel could deal with the cold a lot more easily than a human could, it seemed like.

When the fire was burning and he'd taken a small sip of the water he'd collected from the ship, he sat beside Olivia and brushed her sunlight-colored hair out of her face. His mate, so fragile but so strong at once. She'd never once broken down despite walking into the hellhole and having to kill.

A strange feeling overcame him as he continued to look at his mate, the pale-skinned human female. His tattoo awakened again, glowing and thrumming with a strange intensity. The pain he felt no longer seemed quite so terrible as he watched the female before him.

The female that was his.

He'd already known that she was the one even before he met her, the second his wristband had flashed white and informed him that his match had been found. Then he'd seen her and smelled her and he'd only had his feelings reinforced.

She was his one and only, and he would hold on to her for the rest of his life.

# 7

## OLIVIA

OLIVIA WOKE IN A SUDDEN PANIC. She couldn't move. She felt trapped, as if her arms and legs had been tied together, and her whole body ached. She flailed a little, her head throbbing, and immediately a pair of strong, masculine hands landed on her shoulders.

"You're okay," a deep voice said. It took her a moment to realize it was Kraev. Everything came back to her in a rush and, despite the fact that it should have made her panic more, she relaxed into his touch. "You're just wrapped in a parachute. You were freezing."

She pushed the parachute off her, feeling a slight chill but needing to free her arms to stop feeling so claustrophobic. She would wrap herself back up once she'd adjusted.

She took in their surroundings and saw that they were in a small cave. Dripstones decorated the ceiling and a small fire was burning in the middle. The cave wasn't large by any means, but it wasn't so compact that they couldn't move inside it either. She peeked toward the entrance and could tell that night had fallen on the planet. They were easily out of view of any ships that happened to fly past.

"Where are we? What happened?"

She remembered the Suhlik at the teleport base. She remembered taking off in a spaceship, and the crash, but then...

"We crashed in the mountains," Kraev said, poking a stick into the small fire. It was giving off a surprising amount of heat and Olivia leaned forward. "The impact knocked us both out, but once I woke up, I brought you to this cave. We should be safe here for the night."

Olivia nodded and the movement made her head spin. She raised her hand to her forehead and shut her eyes for a moment. The throbbing moved to her ears and Kraev's voice faded out for a second.

"Are you okay?" he asked, clearly noticing her discomfort. He moved closer to her again, resting his hands on her shoulders. Olivia could see the agitated swish of his tail behind him.

"My head hurts," she said slowly.

She'd already been bashed about by the Suhlik in the base, but she was sure the heavy landing had done her no favors. She might have had a concussion, but it was infinitely harder to diagnose yourself than someone else. Especially a head injury.

"Here." He pulled a small metallic box toward him and clicked it open. Digging inside, he took out a round pill and handed it to her.

She took it but didn't immediately pop it into her mouth. The pill looked strange. Not like any medicine she'd ever seen before. It was shiny purple and it seemed like there was some fluorescent liquid swirling inside it.

"What is this?"

"It numbs the pain," Kraev said. "It'll help with your head. And your ankle. I don't know how bad that is now."

Just the mention of it directed Olivia's attention away from the throbbing in her head to the throbbing in her ankle. She grimaced.

"Not great. I think I made it worse by running on it," she admitted, testing the ankle with her hand. "Well, it's not broken at least. It'll heal."

He leaned forward to pass her some water to take the pill with, and that was when she caught sight of the state he was in.

"Stars," she whispered. His clothes were torn and

he was covered in cuts, some of them deep and bleeding. "You're hurt. Far worse than I am. Why didn't you say anything?"

She swallowed the pill quickly without the water and then grabbed the box he'd retrieved it from. She hoped it was a first aid kit and she was right.

He shook his head. "It's not as bad as it looks. I think I hit some rocks when landing, but I heal more quickly than you, anyway. I'm just glad you weren't seriously hurt in the crash. In a couple of days, these will be practically gone."

"A couple of days is far too long for you to be walking around with open wounds," she said, even though she had no idea if it was true. He knew how his body worked better than she did, but she needed to do *something* and she was good at this. At least she would be helping now, after having been a weight around his neck so far.

"Please, let me help."

Maybe it was the tone of her voice or the desperate expression on her face, but her plea seemed to work. Kraev silently lifted his tattered tunic over his head, revealing more of the tattoos that splayed across his skin, and muscles that she'd only ever seen in what she assumed were airbrushed photos in women's magazines.

Olivia blushed at the sight, swallowing thickly.

She looked inside the first aid kit to see what she'd have to work with. She had no idea how Mahdfel medicine worked. She was sure that their faster healing and improved technology would mean that their hospitals were kitted out with some impressive things, but the first aid kit looked surprisingly rudimentary.

There were bandages and antiseptic wipes, and a needle and thread, both sealed in sterile packages. There were a couple of packets of rubber gloves and some strange-looking pills of different colors.

She smiled at the contents. This was something she could work with. More so than if there had been some fancy Mahdfel tech. She pulled the antiseptic wipes from the kit and opened one up.

"It's going to sting," she warned, even though she was certain he already knew this. Still, it was always better to warn someone, just in case.

Kraev nodded as she placed the wipe on his skin. He didn't react at all as she brushed the wipes over the dozens of cuts on his chest, arms, and back. He sat impassive, his muscles hot and taut beneath her hands. Even his face was emotionless, as if he was doing his best not to react in any way.

Only a slight twitch of his tail and the glowing tattoos on his skin gave any indication of any kind of reaction, and she wasn't too sure that could be called a reaction. Although his tail seemed to occasionally react with his emotions, she'd noticed the tattoos glowing before too, but that seemed to be completely random.

No, it was *she* who was the one doing all the reacting.

Despite her attempts to stay professional and think of him as any other patient, her skin was flushed and her flesh heated under the collar as she swiped over his muscular chest. It was just a physical reaction, she tried to tell herself. A gorgeous, exotic, blue-skinned man who had risked his life for her was there in front of her, shirtless, and she hadn't had sex in years. That was all. Nothing personal, nothing beyond lust.

She'd get over it when the danger was gone and the bigger picture sank in. She was on this hostile mining planet of all places, galaxies away from her home, her family, and her dreams, expected to spend the rest of her life as a glorified babymaker.

Yeah. All that would sink in soon and it wouldn't matter at all how hot the guy was. Any moment now, she'd stop thinking about running her fingers over his chest and pushing him back onto the hard ground of the cave. She'd stop thinking…

She shut her eyes on the thought.

*Stay professional…*

She located the worst of the cuts – the ones that would need stitches – and got to work sewing the gashes back together.

It helped with her indecent thoughts because she had to focus. She desperately didn't want to hurt him more than she had to, but he didn't even react to the needle going in and out of his skin. He just watched her with curious turquoise eyes that she had to stop herself meeting, for fear of her hand faltering in its stitching.

"You seem experienced in this."

The sound of his voice was gruff but neutral. It almost made her jump; she'd been so lost in her thoughts.

"I'm not that experienced," she admitted, finishing the stitching for one wound and cutting the thread. "I'm– I was in medical school. I wasn't qualified yet."

Kraev cocked an eyebrow at her. "You want to become a doctor?"

"Yeah. That was always my dream." She sat back a little, putting down her needle and thread and chewing on the inside of her lip.

Did she actually want to tell him this? She fingered the bracelet around her wrist and remembered Kraev's expression when he'd torn the Suhlik away from her. He'd been full of fury and hatred. He hated the Suhlik as much as she did, she was sure of that.

His brows pulled together. "What is it?"

"I was still young when the Suhlik invaded Earth. I was best friends with the girl who lived next door to me. We were the same age. We used to play games all the time, but our favorite was doctors and nurses. It's kind of silly, I know, but we were just kids." She smiled as she remembered the good times, back when there had been no aliens. Her smile slipped when she thought of what had happened next.

"When the Suhlik attacked, they used gas in my neighborhood. I was out of town then, visiting my grandparents. I got lucky…" She paused briefly, the memories still painful so many years later. "Tammy wasn't as lucky. She was at home just as the attack happened. She breathed in too much of the gas, and I had to watch her waste away and die over the next three days. I was only nine. I shouldn't have had to see that. It shouldn't have ever happened. But it did, and that's why I wanted to become a doctor. For her. For people like her."

She glanced away from him and played with the bracelet again.

Fingertips brushed softly over her wrist and she swallowed thickly, heat spreading like wildfire over her skin. He slipped his fingers between the bracelet and her arm and peered more closely at it. She wondered if he had any idea what he was doing to her. She wondered *why* this was doing so much for her.

"This was hers?" he asked and he sounded so close that she didn't dare to look up at him in case she couldn't stop herself leaning forward and closing the gap.

"Yeah. She gave it to me before she died. I'll never take it off again."

"It's beautiful."

Her lip quirked. "Yeah, it is." It was only a cheap little thing. Tammy had probably bought it at the dollar store. Part of Olivia was surprised it hadn't fallen apart yet, but it was the most important thing in the world that she owned.

"The Suhlik are vicious," Kraev said, squeezing her wrist before pulling his hand back. She finally dared to look at him, but he wasn't looking at her anymore. He stared into the fire.

"My father was the Warlord of his clan," he said. "He died in a battle against the Suhlik. Proudly. He was a Warlord to the end. He knew it was a possibility that he would lose his life that way because of the path he chose, but it's the people who don't choose whose deaths are the most painful. Like your friend. And like mine. Zevyk lost his entire family to a Suhlik attack when he was young."

Olivia sucked in a breath. "That's awful."

It was a story she'd heard a thousand times before on Earth, but it never stopped being any more painful. Somehow, knowing that the Suhlik had the same impact on other planets that they'd had on Earth made everything worse. It wasn't just one planet and people that the lizards had affected. They'd ruined lives all across the galaxy.

"It is," he agreed. He turned back to her and looked at her with strong turquoise eyes. "My people would be proud to have you among them to help. You could complete your medical training here."

She looked up at him sharply. "What?" she asked, so surprised that she made it sound like an accusation rather than the pure shock she was feeling. She hurried to correct herself, "You'd really let me do that?"

Kraev frowned. "If that is what you wish, of course. Medical professionals are always needed and I can already tell you would be great at it." He gestured to the wound that she'd sewn up.

Olivia stared at him dumbly. "But I thought I was supposed to just sit at home and make babies."

Kraev burst into laughter, revealing his sharp,

fanged teeth. His tail lashed on the ground as he guffawed and the mirth lit up his entire face.

For a second, Olivia was speechless. He really was incredibly gorgeous. She'd wondered whether it would even be possible to find an alien attractive, but she'd definitely answered that question for herself. Despite being blue, horned, and having a tail, Kraev was the most attractive man she'd ever set eyes on.

He grinned at her. "Plenty of mates work if they want to. But I definitely want lots of babies."

Olivia turned scarlet and tried not to analyze the tugging in her gut telling her to wrap her arms around him and get closer– a lot closer – to him right there on the floor of the cave. She turned away from him, embarrassed at what she had just implied.

*And what he had implied...*

## 8

### KRAEV

KRAEV WAS LIVING IN TORTURE.

Perfect, glorious torture.

His mate was gorgeous and she was right there, touching his naked chest and looking at him with those big dark eyes. He wanted to roll her onto the floor of the cave and make her truly his right then and there. It took every bit of his willpower to keep himself in check and not just do that.

When she looked away from him, her cheeks turning a captivating pink, the temptation was nearly overwhelming. He'd waited his entire life to find his mate, and she was everything he could have dreamed of and more.

If it weren't for the Suhlik, they wouldn't be trapped in a cave in the middle of the mountains with nothing for miles around. They would be wrapped up in bed together and he would be exploring every inch of what he knew would be a beautiful, curvy body beneath her clothes. His tattoos throbbed at the mere idea of it.

"Why do they do that?" Olivia asked, gesturing to his tattoos as they glowed a fluorescent light in the dimness of the cave. She reached out, almost touching his skin before pulling back.

Kraev wouldn't have minded the touch, but he agreed it was for the best that she didn't. He didn't know why he'd expected her to know more about the Mahdfel than she apparently did, but it looked like she knew near to nothing about them or their culture.

"They glow whenever I'm aroused," he said, resisting the urge to touch her. "Or near you, my mate."

Her cheeks flushed a deep red at his words, even darker than before. He already loved it when she did that. He'd quickly figured out that it meant she was aroused and maybe a little embarrassed.

He supposed he didn't know that much about human culture, either. He would have to fix that. He wanted to know more about her kind, but more importantly, he wanted to know more about her and what her life had been like on Earth.

"Oh," she said in a small voice, reacting to his words with a slight delay.

She ran her hand over the back of her neck, breathing a little heavier.

Watching her made his cock hard in his pants and his tail twitched. He hoped it wasn't too obvious to her. As much as he wanted her to know how much he desired her, they were currently in the midst of danger.

She moved away from him a little, and he refused to let it sting. She was just concerned for their safety, like he was.

"Don't worry," he said. "I'm not going to risk getting distracted. When I claim you, it'll be when we're safe, in my home, in my bed."

Olivia turned redder still. "Yeah. When we're safe," she repeated, but he couldn't place the tone in her voice. "Then things will go back to normal."

She shifted a little as she sat and her sweet scent wafted into his nose, stronger than before. She was wet between her thighs; he was certain of it. He wanted to bury his face between her legs and taste her, watch her writhe and moan because of him.

"You should get some sleep," he said, his voice gruff. His tail swished behind him and he was well aware of how much more intensely his tattoos were glowing. She couldn't look away from them. The more he continued to think about her, the more difficult it was to resist his more primal urges. "We're going to need to start walking when the fighting dies down."

She winced, glancing at her ankle. "I'm not sure how much walking I'm going to be able to manage."

"We'll figure something out."

She smiled, and he didn't know why, but she lay down beside the fire and pulled the parachute over her like a blanket. "I'm glad you don't think I'm useless," she said.

Kraev looked at her like she was crazy. "Of course I don't think you're useless." Even if she hadn't proven that she could hold her own against the Suhlik, he would have never thought she was useless. She was his mate. She was perfect, and that included being her own woman.

He had no idea where she'd got the impression that he would be locking her in a room and preventing her from living her life. Females were just as important in Mahdfel culture as males, just for different reasons. They weren't lesser. They weren't beneath the men.

He hoped he would be able to show her that.

She fell asleep quickly, and he watched the rise and fall of her chest with peace in his heart that he hadn't felt in years. He could have sat and watched her all night, but like he'd said, he wasn't going to risk getting distracted by her. He'd already spent too long inside the cave. He needed to make sure that the Suhlik hadn't realized they had survived the crash. If the Suhlik knew, they could be hunting them down right now.

He brushed fingers over her cheek and whispered, "I'll make sure you're safe, *leani*."

He went to stand at the entrance of the cave, with his hand on the butt of his gun.

In the sky above the mountains, the battle was still raging fiercely. He could see Mahdfel and Suhlik ships alike, shooting close quarters and long-range missiles that lit up the dark sky.

For the first time since they'd crashed, he allowed himself to wonder what had happened to Zevyk. He hoped his brother was still alive, that he'd managed to fix whatever had happened like he normally did.

Fighting the urge to lay down next to Olivia and hold her close to stave off the danger that surrounded them, Kraev stood guard at the edge of the cave, his body stiff and his back to his mate so that she could sleep peacefully. He never wanted her to have to worry as long as he was there.

# 9

## OLIVIA

OLIVIA WOKE UP WITH A CHILL. She was still wrapped in the parachute and the fire was still radiating some heat. Kraev must have kept it going while she slept, but it wasn't enough to ward off the wind that had started whistling into the cave. She hoped it would calm down soon.

She looked up at the thought of Kraev and saw her match standing in the doorway to the cave, tense as he watched the sky. Based on the amount of light, it seemed to be nearly morning.

"Still fighting?" she asked.

The sudden sound of her voice didn't seem to startle him. Instead, he just nodded. "Yes. Still fighting." He turned to her. "Did you sleep well? You didn't seem to be moving around much."

"Well enough," she said. The ground had been a

bit hard to fall asleep on, but once she was asleep, she slept like a log. It was a special talent of hers. "I have no idea how long I slept for."

"Long enough that you should feel rested." He moved away from the mouth of the cave and came to sit beside her next to the fire.

Having him next to her immediately warmed her chilled body a little bit. She wanted to curl into his embrace and accept that warmth properly. She immediately chastised herself for the though and wrapped her arms around her middle instead.

"Hungry?" he asked, misinterpreting her gesture.

Now that he'd mentioned it though, her stomach rumbled. "Actually, yes. Starving. I can't remember the last time I didn't eat for this long."

He grabbed a bag from beside the fire and retrieved two bars in what looked like white candy wrappers. He handed one to her and took one for himself.

Dare she hope for chocolate?

Olivia eagerly opened the packaging, but what she found inside was definitely not chocolate. Or any candy that she recognized for that matter. It was a smooth bar of… something. It was deep turquoise like the color of Kraev's eyes and the consistency was a little squidgy. She tried not to look too skeptical about it and took a hearty bite. Her nose wrinkled.

It tasted strange. Not *bad* but not really like anything she'd had before either. It was thick and dry, with a cookie-like consistency, but it tasted a little bit like how she imagined sawdust would taste.

She was a little relieved when Kraev pulled a similar expression to her own.

"I've never had to eat the emergency rations before," he admitted. "They are… not ideal."

She laughed and grabbed the bottle of water, careful not to drink too much of it. She didn't know whether they'd be able to get any more drinking water. This bar was so dry though that she wasn't going to be able to eat it without a good helping of water.

"They're not so bad," she lied.

He frowned at her. "You don't have to be polite about this terrible food. It's not made to be tasty," he said. "It's pure protein. If we were stuck out here for days or weeks, I wouldn't be complaining, I suppose."

"So, what is food like here?" she asked. "If it's not like this."

"Delicious." He smiled. "We have greenhouses on the planet. They're huge domes in the foothills of the volcano that houses the main base. You can't see them from here – they're on the other side of the mountains – but they grow amazing fruits. You'll like it there, I think. They're one of my favorite places on R-2841."

Olivia liked the idea of huge greenhouses. She'd lived in the suburbs when she was younger and there'd been a lot more greenery than central Minneapolis, which was where she'd ended up while she was in medical school.

"I can't wait to see them," she said.

He grinned at her.

"Is it okay if I go and have a look outside?" she asked. "I mean, not to actually go outside, just to look from the entrance. I haven't seen it properly yet. Your planet."

She thought he was going to say no when he hesitated, but then he nodded. "Okay. I haven't seen anything flying low or in this direction in a while. Just stay as out of sight as you can."

It was only when she went to stand up that the pain in her ankle exploded. She groaned, seeing stars for a moment.

"Dammit," she muttered. "I forgot how bad this thing was. I'd been distracted."

Kraev was immediately by her side, putting a hand on her arm and letting her know that she could put her weight on him if she needed to. She tested her ankle again, and this time, it wasn't quite so bad.

"I think the shock of putting weight on it just surprised me," she said. It still ached, but it wasn't the intense pain that she'd experienced just now. The medicine had probably helped as well. She limped toward the edge of the cave and peered out onto the planet that was now her home, as odd as it felt to think that.

Her breath caught in her throat as she looked out over the foreign world. It was bleak and grey. All she could see were the rocky mountains surrounding them. They disappeared high up into the clouds and formed a deep ravine in the distance. A freezing wind bit at her cheeks and she could barely see a single piece of wildlife as she looked out over what appeared to be endless snow and ice. Yet, it was oddly beautiful.

"This is the first time I've been out in the mountains," Kraev said, coming up behind her. "There's no reason to, normally. I've only seen it from above before, on a ship. But it's actually quite beautiful out here."

"It really is," she replied, leaning closer to him before she could stop herself. It was just for warmth, she told herself. Kraev seemed to constantly radiate heat and it was only natural for her to seek it in the freezing weather.

Still, a part of her couldn't help but wish that Kraev would wrap his arms around her while they watched over the icy scenery.

"Not that this is how I planned things going when I got my match," he muttered.

Unable to resist, she turned to him and asked, "What was your plan? If everything had gone perfectly?"

"I have a gift in my quarters," he said, looking at her in the eye. "I've had it for years, waiting for when I'd be matched. Now, because I haven't given it to you straight away, I'm worried that it isn't good enough."

Warmth invaded Olivia at his thoughtfulness. He'd gotten her a gift. It was so sweet. This wasn't what she'd been expecting from her Mahdfel match at all. He wasn't rough or harsh or insistent on keeping her locked away. She'd thought that becoming a Mahdfel bride would be horrifying, that she'd be matched to some brute and forced to make babies.

But her match actually seemed kind. He was sweet and strong, and he seemed desperate to please her. It was rather endearing.

The realization that she actually liked him hit her

like a train. It shouldn't have. She'd spent the last few hours before sleeping trying not to throw herself at him, but that had just been lust. She hadn't thought she *liked him*. But she did. She actually wanted to spend time with him. She liked just sitting and talking to him.

If only he was on Earth and not here, on this desolate planet that the Suhlik were so determined to take control of. She could be back with her family and her career and he could become a part of her world. There was still fighting to do against the Suhlik back on Earth. Or at least, the planet needed to be protected. He could transfer there, right?

Yet, she knew that wasn't how it worked.

"I'm sure whatever your gift is, it'll be perfect," she said with a smile. "It's nice of you to have gotten me something."

The tattoos on his skin flared to life and his turquoise eyes glittered as he gazed at her. "It's a tradition on Raewan," he explained. "The male always gives their mate a gift, to show his commitment to her. To show that he can take care of her."

Olivia smiled, blushing slightly at the glow of his tattoos. "Well, you've definitely taken care of me so far," she replied. "Keeping me alive is the biggest gift you could have given."

"You helped keep me alive too. Is that an Earth tradition?"

It took her a moment to realize he was teasing her. She chuckled. "I'd like to avoid any traditions that involve us nearly dying."

They both turned back to the entrance to the cave and Kraev pointed up toward the sky. "The battle seems to be dying down," he said. "We should start moving. I can go for a while without food, but I don't think you'd fare as well. Besides, the wreckage of the ship is clearly visible. If we're unlucky, Suhlik might track us by using it. We should get as far away from here as possible."

Olivia nodded. "Okay." But she was worried about her ankle. Descending through the snowy foothills wasn't going to be easy walking and she wasn't sure she could have managed a lot of walking even on flat, even ground. The medicine might help with the pain, but that didn't mean it was smart to put weight on her foot. "We'll see how it goes."

She looked longingly at the fire and the parachute that had barely kept her warm last night. She wasn't looking forward to this walk at all. But Kraev had seemed so confident that she could manage it, and she wanted to live up to his expectations of her.

She limped back inside the cave and sat down by

the medical kit. She took another one of the pain killers and pulled out some bandage material, wrapping it around her ankle. She hoped it would provide some much-needed support for the walk, but she knew it wouldn't be much help.

"I'm going to melt some snow over the fire so we can get some more water to drink," Kraev said, "and then we'll set off."

Thankfully, he picked up the parachute and loaded it into a bag on his back as best as he could, and brought the rest of the rations they had with them. The first aid kit and the drinking water he'd just melted came too.

She felt terrible looking at him loaded up with all those things. He hadn't put his torn shirt back on and she could clearly see his muscles bulge under the weight. He was obviously a thousand times stronger than her, but he was also still covered in wounds. While they were obviously healing faster than they would have on any human, it didn't mean seeing the gashes became any easier.

"Do you want me to carry anything?" she asked, leaning against the wall of the cave to take the weight off her ankle.

"Of course not," he replied. "You're injured. It's going to be tough enough as it is."

She couldn't really argue with that, so they

started out as they were. She stuck as close beside him as she could, feeling unsteady on the rocky ground. The painkiller did its job surprisingly well. It held the worst of the pain away, but her ankle was still unreliable at best.

From the cave, she'd been able to see some of the landscape, but now that they were outside and the sun was higher in the sky, she could properly appreciate what she'd missed in the semi-darkness of the morning.

The moons were everywhere. There must have been fifteen of them that she could see in the sky, all of various sizes, though she wasn't sure if that was because they were further or closer away, or just because they *were* different sizes.

And then there was the landscape. As bleak and hostile as it had looked, in the light of day, she could see the slight blue tint to the snow that covered the ground. She could also see settlements in the ravine that she hadn't noticed before. Or were they settlements? They were just too far away for her to discern the shapes.

"What's that?" she asked Kraev, gesturing toward them.

"That's a mining rig," he replied. "One of the farthest ones out. The main volcano base and the other volcanic areas on the planet are the biggest sources of hellstone, but there are smaller concentrations all across the planet. We are always on the lookout for more."

Olivia squinted in the direction of the rigs, trying to see better. "Do people live there?"

Kraev shook his head. "There's not really any need to actually force people to go out and live on the rigs or spend all their days there. All our mining is done by machinery and it's monitored from our base in the volcano. We simply collect the hellstone whenever there's enough of it. We haven't had a problem with the equipment since we discovered the hellstone here and that was nearly four decades ago."

Olivia whistled, and secretly thought, *Well, that's due a disaster then.* Out loud, she said, "A volcano base sounds pretty cool. I used to be fascinated by volcanoes when I was younger."

"There are no volcanoes near my home," Kraev replied. "Living in one was a bit scary at first."

"You? Scared?" she asked in disbelief.

He grinned. "Suhlik are predictable. Nature, not so much."

Olivia chuckled. She couldn't argue with that.

# 10

## KRAEV

KRAEV SLOWED his pace considerably as they started down some of the steeper declines that would lead them onto the icy tundra in front of them. He was on high alert, watching out for possible dangers around them and ready to catch Olivia the second she looked unstable.

He hated that his mate was injured, but a part of him couldn't help but also be proud of her. She was doing surprisingly well despite her injured ankle. She clearly knew the importance of staying on the move. Although the ankle clearly caused her discomfort even after taking the medicine, she didn't complain once.

It bothered Kraev how out in the open they were. Ships were still in the skies, even if the battle wasn't raging as brutally as it had been. A Suhlik ship could easily spot them out here in the foothills without any cover, and if it was him versus a ship, he knew there was no chance of him coming out the victor.

He constantly kept one eye on the sky and one on his mate.

When they hit a rather flat stretch, he stopped and offered Olivia a bottle of water and another painkiller. They were nearly out of the medicine, but she looked like she was struggling more and more. Her light hair was tousled around her face and perspiration shone on her skin.

She took the bottle eagerly, flashing him a strained grin. "Thanks."

His chest ached at the pained expression on her face.

"Do you want me to carry you for a bit?"

She flushed, looking uncertainly at him. "You're already carrying so many things."

"I am quite strong," he teased, hoping to gain a smile from her, but the words had no effect. She looked completely exhausted, and once they'd stopped, he could tell that she was shivering in the cold weather.

Yet, she didn't want him to carry her. Somewhere deep inside, that knowledge hurt him. She had shied away from him at the teleport base too, hadn't wanted him to touch her. Had he done something wrong? Did his mate dislike him?

At the same time, Kraev had realized that it was important for his human mate to feel useful. In her eyes, she was probably dragging him down right now, as if she ever could. What she didn't understand was that carrying his mate would never be a problem for him.

"We are too out in the open right now," Kraev said, changing tactics. His mate was exceptionally intelligent, and although he didn't want to worry her, maybe logic would work on her instead. "We should move as quickly as possible, and there may be paths further ahead where it will not be possible for me to carry you. It would be good to give your ankle a rest when you can."

Olivia glanced down at her ankle, then at the backpack on his back, clearly still hesitant. "Let me wear the backpack and then you can carry me," she finally said.

Kraev smiled. His mate was stubborn. It amused him, because he was stubborn too. The fates really had matched him with the most perfect female for him.

He handed the backpack to Olivia, and she huffed as she took it from him. Kraev's heart jumped as she nearly tripped under its weight trying to put it on. He immediately rushed to her side, grabbing the backpack from her. It was clearly too heavy for her.

"It's– It's fine," she said, still holding onto the backpack. "I'm just going to take the parachute out, okay? We don't need it."

"No." Kraev shook his head. She was already shivering in the current weather and he knew the nights in the mountains would be even colder. "Let me take the backpack. I can carry it across my chest and you on my back. It will be fine."

The look his mate gave him nearly pierced his heart. Her brown eyes were wide and she looked close to tears. She was cold, in pain, and out of strength. Guilt filled him at not being able to care for her more properly.

"It will be fine," he repeated, brushing his fingers against Olivia's cheek. "Please, Olivia. Let me have it."

Finally, she seemed to relent. She let go of the backpack and Kraev swung it across his chest. He knelt down so that Olivia could climb onto his back and, hesitantly, her fingers wrapped around his shoulders. Her body was tense but warm against his. He still hadn't put on his ruined shirt, and though she was clothed, he loved the feel of her against his naked back.

After making sure he had a good grip on her and

that she was comfortable, he started walking down the flat terrain. At last, she began to relax.

"You're warm," she mumbled against his back. "Maybe this carrying thing was a good idea, after all."

Kraev chuckled, pleased that she was feeling better. "I only have good ideas," he said.

Olivia laughed and the pleasant timbre of it made the tattoos on his body tingle. She clearly noticed their glow, because she traced a finger across the one on his shoulder.

"What are the tattoos of?" she asked.

"They're tattoos of the battles I've fought," he said. "I know it's not obvious from looking at them, but when a battle happens, a specific symbol is created to signify victory or bravery in that fight." He gestured to the one on his shoulder that she had touched. "This was a previous battle on R-2841. I was the pilot with the most Suhlik ships destroyed."

"That's amazing," Olivia said. She kept touching the tattoos on his arms, tracing the intricately woven lines with her fingers, and he couldn't help the shivers that coursed through his body at her gentle caress. The tattoos started to glow brighter and his tail swished in pleasure. "You'll have to tell me about them all one day."

Kraev closed his eyes at her touch. In his mind,

he could picture her lying in their bed, picking out tattoos and asking him what they meant while she traced them with her fingers. Or her lips.

"I'll do that," he replied, his voice gruff.

His tail kept swooshing behind him, twitching to wrap around Olivia's leg, but he wasn't certain she would appreciate the intimate touch. Besides, he needed to stay focused. He looked up to the sky and kept walking down the slope, trying to keep his thoughts in check.

He focused on their environment and ignored the soft curves of his mate pressed against his back, until a sound in the distance made him pause. He turned in the direction of the sound and saw a small, dark spot between the clouds.

"There's a ship coming," he said, nodding toward the skies. He couldn't tell whether it was a Suhlik ship or a Mahdfel ship yet, but he knew he couldn't be too careful. He started to jog toward a slight outcrop of rock that he'd noticed in the mountain. Hopefully, they could hide underneath it.

"That's a ship?" Olivia asked, squinting at the skies as he set her down on the ground beneath the outcrop. "How can you tell?"

"I've spent years flying in these skies. You learn to recognize the sound of a spaceship, no matter how far."

Her brown eyes grew concerned. "Is it Suhlik?"

He shook his head. "I can't tell yet. It's better to stay hidden until I know for sure. With any luck, it's a rescue ship sent to find us."

Olivia nodded, but Kraev felt her body tense. He wasn't sure he believed the bit about a rescue ship either, not with his wristband communicator broken. Minutes passed by as they waited for the ship to fly closer and he kept peeking up at the skies. When the ship finally flew close enough for him to see it properly, his heart froze.

"It's Suhlik," he said under his breath. "Stay hidden."

The fact that a Suhlik ship had gotten this far and was flying freely without any Mahdfel ships around was bad news. Olivia seemed to realize this too. She sucked in a breath and huddled closer to him. Kraev wrapped his arm around her in comfort. Hopefully, the ship wouldn't see them from here.

They stayed huddled together for several minutes until the ship finally passed over them. A heavy breath escaped Olivia's lungs.

"Are we good to go now?" she asked.

Kraev shook his head. "Sensors could notice our movements at this distance still," he said. "We need to give it a few more minutes until the ship is focused elsewhere."

Olivia nodded and remained in her place. After a while, she suddenly asked, "Did you always want to be a pilot?"

"Yes," he replied without hesitation. "Ever since I first entered my warrior training as a child, there was something about being in a ship – and in space – that always appealed to me. Maybe it was because it meant not normally having to deal with the Suhlik up close and personal. I get to keep their ugly faces out of sight and focus on blowing up their ships instead."

Olivia chuckled. "I can see why that would be appealing. Yesterday was definitely too close to comfort on the 'up close and personal with the Suhlik' front." She shivered at the memory, and Kraev pulled her tighter against his chest.

"You'll never get that close to one again as long as I can help it," he replied.

He hated how close the Suhlik had gotten to her. Their security measures on the planet had failed at the most crucial moment and he had nearly lost his mate before he'd even met her.

His blood boiled at the thought. He was going to have words with the Warlord about that.

As if sensing his turmoil, Olivia moved even closer to him, pressing her hand against his chest. She looked up at him, straight into the eyes, and he was taken aback by the unmistakable trust in her gaze. She hadn't trusted him when they'd met. She had been suspicious of him even still in the cave. But now, it felt like something had shifted.

"I know you'll keep me safe," she said, her voice speaking of that same trust.

Kraev vowed to never break that trust for as long as he lived.

# 11

## OLIVIA

OLIVIA HAD NEVER THOUGHT that she'd actually feel safe against the Suhlik. She'd lived in abject terror of them ever since the invasion of Earth, certain that they'd return and take her one day, like she'd gotten away from them when she wasn't supposed to.

But here, even though this was by far the most real danger she'd been in since that first day the Suhlik had entered her world, she didn't feel that fear. She felt safe. Protected. She knew that Kraev would let nothing bad happen to her. It was the strangest feeling, and she couldn't really explain to herself why she trusted him that much. Just that she did.

Several more minutes passed before the sound of

the enemy ship finally disappeared. They emerged from beneath the outcrop. Olivia immediately moaned in pain as the throbbing in her ankle increased. Crouching low beneath the rock had done her no favors.

"Are you alright?" Kraev asked, his expression concerned.

"I'll be fine," Olivia said, pressing her arm against his chest for support. She could feel the steady rising and falling of his heartbeat beneath his muscular chest, and the tattoos on his skin lit up brighter.

Now knowing the meaning behind the fluorescent light, her cheeks flushed at the reaction. She quickly pulled her hand away and turned to the sky. She could no longer see the Suhlik ship that had passed above them and she was grateful for that.

"We should get going again," Kraev said. "There's still plenty of daylight left."

Olivia nodded. She let him hoist her onto his back, wrapping her arms and legs around him again – as well as her limbs could wrap around his large, muscled body – and absorbed the heat he was putting out. She was cold, but he managed to be boiling despite being still shirtless. If it came down to it at night, she wouldn't be opposed to huddling against him for warmth.

Kraev carried her as they continued to descend the mountain, but they soon came to a steep cliff face and there was no way that Kraev could carry her down. Instead, he set her back on the ground and they made slow progress on their own feet. Her ankle burned, but she knew they couldn't stop in the middle of the rocks, so she ignored the pain.

By the time they got to the bottom – and it was a good thing that another ship hadn't come nearby, because there was no way that they could have moved anywhere fast enough to shield them – she was breathing heavily.

"I can't do anymore," she said, collapsing down onto a rock that wasn't buried in ice and lifted her leg up so it was elevated. "It's really hurting now."

Kraev immediately rushed over and wrapped his hand around her ankle softly, checking the joint slowly to make sure that he wasn't hurting her. His deep turquoise eyes were etched in concern. "I don't want to make it worse."

"I don't think it's getting worse," she said. "It's just that using it so much is making it ache and throb more. I just need to keep it elevated for a while." Her stomach rumbled. "And I'm getting a little hungry too, I guess."

Kraev nodded. He looked around at where they'd

stopped. "Okay. We can stop nearby for the night. I just need to find somewhere that'll keep us sheltered and out of sight." The wind was starting to pick up, but the exertion from walking for so long was staving off the cold for now.

Olivia hated being left on her own for those ten or so minutes, even though she knew Kraev was nearby. She was on a strange planet and she had no idea what kind of creatures crawled in the dark.

When Kraev finally returned and hoisted her into his arms so that she didn't have to strain her ankle any more, she relaxed into his hold. Already, the chill was getting to her again and having him carry her bridal style was like being wrapped in a nice warm blanket.

She wished he was actually wrapped around her.

The cave was a lot smaller this time, but it would still keep them out of sight of the sky. It had only a small opening that Kraev had to crouch to enter through. Inside, he had already deposited their supplies.

"I'll get a fire going before it gets dark," he said.

Light was barely filtering in through the small entrance and the sun had nearly set. Olivia could see the several moons high up in the sky again. Kraev handed her the parachute from the backpack and she wrapped it around herself again. She watched him work with her knees pulled up to her chest to try and keep warm even though she knew she should be elevating her ankle.

"I hope the volcano base is warmer," she said, her teeth chattering.

"It is," Kraev said. "It's the only place on the planet that's properly warm. It's why the greenhouses are out there, too."

She shook her head. "I can't imagine growing up on a planet like this. How did you live?"

Kraev burst into laughter. "Stars, I'm not from here."

"Why is that so funny?" she asked with a frown, feeling a little offended. Maybe there was some obvious cultural heritage that she'd missed because of her ignorance. Kraev had spoken of home, but somehow, she had assumed that home meant *here*.

He seemed to realize he'd offended her and held out a placating hand. "Just because there's nothing really here. I don't know. I guess it's because it's so different from my home planet. You weren't wrong to assume. There are plenty of young warriors on R-2841 now who were born here."

"So where were you born?"

"I was born on Raewan. It's a planet in the same

galaxy as R-2841. I suppose it has a similar story to yours, only ours began many decades before yours. The Suhlik came and the Mahdfel came to rescue the planet. The Raewani people were very primitive then and the traditional culture is still strong even among the Mahdfel on the planet." He went quiet, looking into the fire in thought. "I have not been on Raewan in years."

"Do you have family there?" she asked, leaning forward as she listened to him speaking.

She knew nothing about his culture, but she was very interested to learn as much as possible. It was so different and yet the story was so similar. She wondered if the colorful tunic and pants he wore were a part of that traditional culture he'd mentioned.

She half-regretted not having learned more about the Mahdfel and the many other planets they traded with. She'd had a strong desire to stay as far away from all things extra-terrestrial for as long as she could. Yet, a part of her wouldn't have wanted to hear this from anyone's lips but Kraev's.

"I do." He smiled now, clearly thinking of his family. "My mother and six brothers."

"Six!" she said, her eyes widening in surprise. "So many kids!" She couldn't even imagine what it must be like to have such a large family.

"And that's not including Zevyk, who is basically my brother too." He grinned, looking satisfied with himself. It was clear that he loved his family very much.

"Are you close?" she asked. If he hadn't been back to see them in years, she wondered how close they *could* be. She saw her parents and brother every week.

But then again, they lived in the same city, just a thirty-minute drive from each other. It wasn't difficult to see them.

"Very. I know it might not seem like it."

She flushed, knowing she must have given away her thoughts on her face. "Sorry," she interrupted. "I wasn't judging. Just curious."

"We are close, but we all have our own lives and obligations. R-2841 is under constant threat from the Suhlik, but Raewan is living in prosperity for now. When the Warlord in charge of R-2841 requested more warriors for this location, I immediately signed up. Staying here and keeping Raewan – and the rest of the universe – safe by not letting the Suhlik get hold of the hellstone is where my duties lay."

He shuffled a little closer to her as she continued to shiver, and wrapped an arm around her shoulders. The heat was instant and welcome, and she leaned into his arms.

"But maybe now that I have my mate, I'll take some time and go see my family. We can take some time," he corrected. "My number one duty now is to make sure that my family is happy. And now, you are my family."

Heat flooded her cheeks at his words. "I would like to see your home planet," she admitted. "And I hope that you could visit my home planet one day, too." Was that even possible? "I have a younger brother. And my parents are both still well, living in my home town."

With how everything had gone after being sent to this planet, she hadn't had much time to think about her family. But now that she did, tears threatened to spill forth from her eyes. She cleared her throat, pushing the thoughts of her family aside.

"But of course, I don't want you to abandon your duty if that's what's important."

She already felt bad that he was out here in the mountains, caring for her, when he could have been fighting the Suhlik. Duty seemed so important to him and she was keeping him away from that. The thought of him out there in danger made her increasingly uncomfortable though. The more time she spent with him, the closer she grew to him.

If he ended up like Tammy, she wasn't sure how she would cope. She wasn't sure she wanted to get attached to someone who might just die soon. It was a thought she was pushing to the back of her mind and trying to ignore. There were no Suhlik with them now, just the two of them learning about each other, skin-to-skin and cozy in the small cave.

"I would love to visit your planet and meet your family," he said, his words spreading a new hope and warmth through her. "And I want you to meet my family. I want my sons to know their uncles and their grandparents."

"Sons," she said, feeling a little flush at the idea.

Kids. Already. They were already talking about kids.

It shouldn't have been strange, considering that was the exact reason she had been sent here for. To make little warrior babies with her alien match. But what surprised her was that she was no longer so terrified about the whole idea.

Stars, she was losing it. She needed to backpedal in this relationship, and fast. She had known Kraev for barely twenty-four hours. She needed to–

"*Lots* of sons," he said, squeezing her tight against his chest. Clearly, he was determined not to let the topic go. "Our sons."

Her yawn was well-timed. The conversation had

suddenly gotten too intense for her. Or, more like, the conversation had made her realize how intense her feelings toward Kraev were starting to get, and she was shying away from that. She couldn't have such feelings for him in such a short time… Right? Just days ago, she had thought all Mahdfel were brutes.

"You should get some sleep," Kraev said.

"You're the one who should be sleeping. You didn't get any sleep last night, did you?"

"I need to be awake to watch the entrance, in case any Suhlik manage to track us," he replied, though he made no move to stand at the edge of the cave entrance today like he had yesterday.

She could see it in his posture and his face now that she was looking at him. Lines that had not been there before framed his features, and even his tail was still. He was tired.

"Really," she said. "Please, just get a little bit of sleep. Just a couple of hours."

He dithered, his sparkling turquoise eyes looking hesitantly into hers.

"I'll rest my eyes for a little bit," he conceded at last. "But I can't go to sleep. I won't risk it."

"Okay," she said, knowing a tone of finality when she heard one. She yawned again. "I am going to try and get some sleep though. Wake me if you need anything."

She shimmied down so she was lying beside the fire in the small cave. Forming a pillow from the parachute and draping it over the rest of her, she put down her head and shut her eyes.

She already knew that Kraev and their many sons would be visiting her in her dreams tonight.

## 12

KRAEV

KRAEV HAD BEEN certain that he wouldn't fall asleep. He'd stayed awake for this long before and coped just fine. But soon, he found himself flickering his eyes open and he realized he'd been out cold. He lay on the cool rock floor of the cave, his arms wrapped around Olivia, and he knew that was the reason he'd succumbed to his tiredness.

Sitting with her, he had just been so comfortable and content. He hadn't been as alert as he should have been. He tightened the arms around her waist and shoulder for a moment, taking in the sweet scent of her and the warmth of her body, reveling in her small form nestled against his.

Then, it hit him.

There was a reason he'd woken up now. The fire had gone out, but it didn't look like that had just happened. He looked around the cave and could see nothing different, but a strange sensation crawled up his spine. Something rustled outside the cave, and suddenly, every hair on his body stood on end.

They were being watched.

He turned his head slowly toward the entrance. There was no one in the cave with them, but there were people nearby. He was sure of it.

He had been worried the fire might attract Suhlik to their location, but it hadn't been optional. It was too cold during the nights even though they were sheltered from the brunt of the wind. He would have been okay, but he was terrified that he was going to make Olivia ill if he didn't keep her warm. She was so small and cold.

He untangled himself from her and moved toward the mouth of the cave. He hadn't taken off his weapons belt since the Suhlik had attacked and he rested his hand on the butt of his gun now, just in case he was right and one of the evil creatures did spring out of one of the many hiding places the foothills had to offer.

On the face of it, he couldn't see anything, but his sense of being watched only increased as he stood half-out of the cave and scanned the area. His tail swayed anxiously and his whole body was on high alert.

Staying close to the rock face that the cave entered into, he edged along it to try and get to a vantage point where he would be able to see more. But it was useless. The area they'd stopped in had a lot of large rocks that were plenty big enough to hide a Suhlik behind and there was no way for him to see behind them without getting close.

Switching the gun in his hand for two traditional knives, Kraev forced himself to edge away from the wall and start looking behind the rocks. The dark night was going to give him some cover at least. It might have been reckless, but there was no way he was going to return to the cave and wall himself in there with his mate if there were Suhlik out here. He needed to know for certain.

He kept looking over his shoulder, back at the cave, every few seconds. Nothing was going to sneak past him and get at Olivia while he did his investigating.

The first couple of rocks had nothing behind them, but it didn't make him doubt his instincts. His instincts had been right many times before and he was sure he'd been woken up by something.

Then, the second he turned a corner, he saw something move in the darkness. He moved before thinking, springing himself on top of the moving figure – a male – and put the knife to his throat.

It was only afterward, just before he sliced the throat of the threat, that the full situation dawned on him. The light blue skin, the shaved hair and braids, the tribal leather that the male wore over his chest.

His moment of hesitation allowed the other warrior to throw him off. Kraev landed easily on his feet and loosened the grip on his knife.

Then, he grinned.

"Zevyk!" he said, moving toward his brother again, this time to give him a large hug. "Stars, I thought you were Suhlik."

Zevyk laughed. "So little faith, brother," he replied. He gave a whistle and then shouted over his shoulder, "It's Kraev." At normal volume, he asked, "The wreckage to the north is yours?"

"Yes." Kraev walked as he talked, heading back toward the cave entrance and to his mate. "We escaped from the teleport base, but ships followed us. I got one, but another managed to gun us down."

"Us?" Zevyk asked tentatively, keeping pace with Kraev as he walked back to the cave entrance. More warriors emerged from behind rocks and gathered in the clearing in front of the cave. Many of them raised their hands and nodded to acknowledge Kraev.

Olivia's small figure emerged in the mouth of the cave. She was shivering and her eyes were wide with concern. "I wondered where you'd gone," she said softly. "I guess this explains that."

Zevyk clapped Kraev on the back. "I'm happy for you, brother," he said. "I was worried when I didn't hear from you after the teleport base and when I saw you alone just now. I thought maybe you'd lost her."

Kraev wrapped his arms around Olivia, his chest pressing into her back to try to give her some of his warmth. She shivered once but then leaned into his embrace. She still stood a bit lopsided, clearly trying to keep weight off her ankle, but it didn't appear as bad as the day before.

"This is Zevyk," Kraev told her, gesturing to his brother, who was appraising her with blatant curiosity. She was the first human any of the warriors had seen, most likely. "Zevyk, this is Olivia."

Olivia gave him a shy smile. "It's nice to meet you, Zevyk. Thanks for helping us out earlier. And for finding us."

"I'll admit we thought we'd be attacking you rather than saving you, but I'm glad you didn't turn out to be Suhlik that had crashed here." He smiled at Olivia and then turned back to Kraev. "Are both of you okay?" His eyes scanned the wounds on Kraev's chest. "Physically?"

"Olivia's ankle is damaged," Kraev said, ignoring

his own scratches. They were already healing anyway. "She's struggling to walk. I assume you've got a ship nearby?"

Zevyk nodded, his expression gaining a serious edge again. "Not far from here," he said. "Just over the ridge. It won't take long to get there and it's not too difficult walking. You should be able to carry her."

"We're going to continue checking the area," one of the other warriors, a male named Torun, said. "Just to make sure there's nothing we've missed. The Suhlik could have spotted the crashed ship, too."

Zevyk nodded. "I'll take them back to the ship and wait for you there."

Kraev ducked into the cave to grab their supplies and heard Zevyk and Olivia talking outside. He was excited for them to get along. Zevyk was family, and he wanted his mate to know and love all his family as much as he did, because she was part of that family now, too.

He wanted to know her family, too. She spoke so fondly of her parents and her brother. He hoped that one day he would get to meet them.

Outside, he hoisted Olivia onto his back and held her legs with his arms. She rested her chin on his shoulder and was so close to brushing her lips against the skin there that it made his tattoos awaken and his skin shiver.

Zevyk carried what was left of their supplies for them and they headed out toward the ship.

"So," Kraev said to his friend as they walked. "What's the situation? I assume that things have improved if you're out here investigating two-day-old wreckages."

"We've secured the planet's atmosphere," Zevyk replied, walking slightly ahead so that he could lead the way. "But there are Suhlik still on the surface. They got a lot of men down here before we managed to chase their ships off. We're not sure what we're looking at in terms of numbers just yet. That's why the teams are trying to force them out of hiding before they can group up."

Kraev made a noise of distaste. He'd been hoping that things would have been more secure than that. Suhlik still on the planet meant that Olivia was technically still in danger, even if it wasn't immediate. "And the volcano base?"

"Secured. Completely. It was never breached."

Kraev nodded. "Good. Then I can leave Olivia there and she'll be safe."

Olivia's head perked up at that. "Leave me there?" she asked, her voice quiet.

Guilt filled his heart at the uncertainty in her

voice. He didn't want to leave his mate, but he had no choice.

"All the warriors will be on search duty," he said, the statement backed up by a nod from Zevyk. "It's standard procedure. We'll have lost some pilots during the fighting, so my role is doubly important." He squeezed her legs because it was the only place he was holding her, hoping it would comfort her. "Leaving you is the last thing I want to do, but this is my duty."

Olivia was quiet for a while, but finally, she nodded. "That's okay. I understand." Though she didn't sound like she particularly liked it. "Hopefully, one day when you're doing your duty, I'll be in the hospital doing mine."

"I'd like that," he replied. He understood needing purpose, needing to fulfill your duty. It was almost refreshing that he had found a mate who understood that just as much as he did.

"You're a medic?" Zevyk asked, turning to Olivia with a curious expression.

"I was a doctor in training on Earth," she explained. "I'd like to keep training here, if someone is willing to train me."

"I can't see why they wouldn't be. I'm sure Dr. Zayen would like to have more hands in the medical bay."

As they walked, Zevyk and Olivia chatted with each other, and she told him some of the things that Kraev had already heard, about Earth and about herself, and things he had not yet discovered. The conversation set a comfortable mood and warmth filled Kraev's heart. He was getting to know his mate, and his mate was getting to know him and his family.

It looked like things were finally starting to go right.

As Zevyk had said, it wasn't a very long walk to the ship and the ground was easily covered since he carried Olivia. She rested her cheek against his neck as they neared the ship – something much more substantial than the small craft they'd escaped the teleport base on.

"So, what now?" she asked.

"We'll wait for the others in the ship and then we'll fly back to the volcano base. I can show you to my quarters. Your new home. And then I can be debriefed. I'll let you know what I'm doing exactly once that's happened."

She brushed her nose against his neck, her hot breath making him shudder. His tail twitched, tentatively wrapping around her uninjured leg.

"Okay," she said. "That sounds good."

This ship was large enough that it had different

rooms, as well as the bridge, and Olivia looked like she was ready to die of happiness when he showed her to the head.

He moved to the bridge where Zevyk was looking at readouts on the ship's engineering screens. As soon as he came in, his friend turned his full attention to him.

"So, how are you?" Zevyk asked.

Kraev was unable to keep the grin off his face. "I think I might be the happiest man in the universe."

# 13

## OLIVIA

OLIVIA SAT in a seat on the bridge of the ship, with monitors in front of her that were showing information that she didn't understand. Her translator translated the words, but they meant nothing to her. Technical jumbo.

Instead, she watched Kraev as he maneuvered the much larger ship through the skies of R-2841. It really was different with something this big. He regularly turned to call commands to the rest of the crew and communicate with the other pilots. Somehow, watching him take charge of the team made her a little flustered.

She looked out the windows but could see no Suhlik ships in the air. Although the lizards were no doubt hiding somewhere on the surface, the planet looked peaceful.

They arrived in the volcano base after a short flight, landing through a large opening in the mountain wall. Inside, her thoughts immediately gave way to awe.

The base was incredible. It was a masterpiece of engineering that she couldn't imagine in a similar volcano back on Earth. A combination of metal and rock, with a few specks of colorful plants, the volcano formed a massive cave inside its walls. Rings of walkways framed the sides and huge elevators connected each layer. From each level, seemingly hundreds of tunnels led to other areas.

It was a small city.

"Wow," she marveled as they stepped off the ship into a huge hangar and started to walk deeper inside the volcano. The rest of the group splintered off, but Kraev stayed right beside her. "It must have taken ages to build this." She wanted to run her fingers over the silvery metal walls but felt silly.

"I believe it took a couple of years," Kraev said. "It was built before my time. Mostly, the building was done by machines, so it wasn't too arduous. It was figuring out what to tell the machines that was the laborious part, but the Mahdfel architects and engineers in charge were very skilled."

"I can tell that," Olivia said, amazed. She gave in and ran her fingers against the wall they walked beside. It felt like metal. She wasn't sure what she'd been expecting. "It's so quiet here."

They barely ran into anyone as they walked through the base. The corridors were strangely empty considering how big of a structure the volcano was. She'd expected more life inside.

"People are out fighting," Kraev explained. "Well, scouting more than fighting now. It'll take a while to make sure that none of the Suhlik remain on the planet. Even a lone Suhlik could do a lot of harm if people aren't expecting him. And the women and children are most likely in their homes. It's the safest there."

"So, that's where we're going? To your home?"

"Yes." Kraev smiled and she found herself wanting to smile back at him, but her nerves suddenly hit her. This was his home... and hers too, from now on. She wasn't sure what to think of that. Somehow, the reality of that was still yet to hit her. She also wasn't sure what Kraev's expectations were once they got to his rooms...

She blushed at the thought. They were just about to call an elevator when a tall, blue-skinned warrior came up behind them.

"Kraev." He didn't say the name loudly, but his voice commanded attention nonetheless.

Kraev immediately turned and lowered his head. "Warlord," he said.

Olivia hurried to avert her gaze too. She'd been intrigued by the man's extensive number of tattoos and the intricate braiding on his head. He seemed to have more hair than most of the warriors she'd seen so far. Now those things made sense. It must have been a status thing on Raewan.

"I'm glad to see you've returned," the Warlord said to Kraev. "And that you found your mate safely."

"No one is more pleased than me that she is here and healthy." Kraev lifted his head and smiled as he looked the Warlord in the eyes again.

The Warlord turned to her. "You must be Olivia Griffin from Earth. I was notified of your arrival. I'm pleased to see that you are well, despite the circumstances. I'm Rath ek-Tuin, the Warlord in charge of the operation here on R-2841. It's a pleasure to meet you."

Olivia bowed slightly. She wasn't sure what the appropriate protocol was. "It's a pleasure to meet you too... Warlord."

She raised her head and could swear the Warlord's lip had twitched at her addressing him. She might as well have imagined it though because, when he turned back to Kraev, his expression was fully serious.

"I know it's the last thing you want to hear right now, but I'm going to need you on the search teams. A pilot with your skill will be invaluable in rooting out the last of the Suhlik that are hiding on our planet."

Kraev nodded. "I would expect nothing less. I'm ready to do my duty. I want to make sure those lizard scum are off our home."

The Warlord nodded. "Good. Rest tonight. First thing in the morning, I'll give you instructions as to which quadrant you're searching."

"Yes, Warlord," Kraev said, sounding pleased with the outcome.

The Warlord clapped him on the shoulder and then turned and strode away.

Olivia let out a breath she hadn't realized she'd been holding. Somehow, she had completely tensed up in the Warlord's presence.

"So that's the overall boss?" she asked.

Kraev looked like he wanted to disagree with her wording, but eventually nodded. "Yes. He is the current Warlord of the Mahdfel clan on R-2841, but he is very new. The previous warlord died in battle against the Suhlik only a bit over a year ago. He seems to be doing a good job in a bad situation, though."

Olivia nodded. It must not be easy for any of

them in the middle of an invasion.

They took an elevator up six floors and then took one of the corridors off the main ring. Warm lights ran along the roof of the tunnels, illuminating everything without making the metal walls feel too cold and uninviting. At equal intervals, doors lined the corridor on both sides.

They walked deeper into the volcano until Kraev finally came to a stop in front of a door. Olivia's heartrate suddenly spiked. This was it. Her new home.

"I hope it is to your liking," Kraev said almost shyly as he pressed his hand to a panel on the side of the door and it slid open.

Olivia's breath caught in her lungs as she stepped inside his quarters. She hadn't known what to expect from Kraev's room. Maybe something spartan and cold, like the military man's stereotype.

What she found was the opposite of that. The door opened into a small living room, with cushioned seats and a large TV-like screen on the wall. Maps decorated the rest of the walls, depicting a wide array of locations from cities and planets to galaxies and the whole universe. Everything looked sparkling clean and modern, but it was still strangely homey.

She loved it.

"This is nice," she said, looking longingly at the cushioned seats. She hadn't realized how much her back, legs, and ankle were hurting until she looked at something that comfy. Sleeping in caves and straining her ankle had really taken it out of her. She'd never even really hiked back home, never mind done anything like this.

"You like it?" Kraev asked behind her, almost hesitantly.

Olivia smiled at him. "It's a hundred times better than what I was imagining."

He finally cracked a smile, his turquoise eyes sparkling with intensity. "What were you imagining?"

She laughed, rolling her eyes. "You don't want to know. Something like a typical bachelor box or rugged military quarters."

She resisted the urge to slump down onto the softly inviting couch. Instead, she turned to explore the rooms behind the three doors leading off from the living room. One was to a kitchen.

"What's this?" she asked as she walked inside, gesturing to a large device that looked kind of like a microwave. While the room was obviously a kitchen, it looked different to one on Earth, with strange devices all over the place, and she couldn't begin to guess what they were used for.

"That's the food replicator," Kraev said.

She tilted her head, looking at the device. "Food replicator?"

"Yes." He walked closer behind her and opened the cubic machine. "It can create any food in the universe."

Olivia's mouth dropped and she turned to him, her eyes wide. "*What?*" She could still have pizza? Still have ice cream? "Earth food too?" When he nodded, she said, "I can't believe you didn't mention this before!" He'd been singing praises of the greenhouses and fruit but had neglected to mention a machine that could create her a burger?

Kraev laughed. "I'll admit it's useful, but it almost never tastes as good as the real thing. I don't use it *that* often."

"Can I try it?" Suddenly, she felt giddy. And *hungry.* The last thing she'd eaten was one of those terrible protein bars.

"Of course," Kraev said.

He showed her how the replicator worked and she keyed in something simple. A peanut butter and jelly sandwich. It didn't get more classic than that.

The screen blacked out as it created her food and then, in just a couple of minutes, it beeped to signal it was done. She pulled out the plate and looked at the sandwich from every angle. It really did look just right. It looked pretty perfect, even. More perfect than any PB&J she'd ever made herself.

But when she bit into it, she knew what Kraev had meant. It wasn't bad by any stretch of the imagination. It was good, even. It just wasn't quite right. It was like you could taste the artificial flavor to it, just a little. She still moaned in appreciation. After the protein bars, this was the best thing in the world.

"If you think that's good, then come with me," Kraev said with a smirk, linking his arm through hers and guiding her from the kitchen, plate of sandwich still in her hand.

He led her into the bedroom and her eyes were immediately drawn to the bed. It was huge, almost filling the whole room. It was pretty much the only thing in there, apart from a wardrobe built into the wall.

She suddenly felt nervous. What was Kraev up to? Why had he led her here? Impure thoughts raced through her mind and all the temptation she'd felt when they were cuddled in the cave together came roaring back to the surface.

They were here, alone. Safe and sound.

This was when he'd said he'd *claim* her.

It should have made her want to argue against

the idea when he used that word, but all she felt was turned on.

For a change, though, that didn't seem to be what Kraev had on his mind. Instead of pushing her down on the bed and 'claiming' her like he'd promised, he opened his wardrobe and pulled out a woven twig basket. It was quite large, with a lid on top, and strangely at odds with the rest of the décor. She had no idea what to expect.

"Here," he said, lifting the lid. Inside, she could see what looked like crystallized fruits. Most of them were various shades of turquoise and blue, just like the Mahdfel she'd seen on the base. They came in many beautifully intricate shapes and sparkled in a wrapper at the bottom of the basket. One of them looked like a flower.

"What are they?" she asked, not wanting to touch one in case she damaged them.

"They're sweets," he said, pushing the box closer toward her. "I realize keeping fruit in my closet may not be the most standard thing, but I wanted to keep them close to me. They're important. I brought them from Raewan when I came here. I wanted to give them to my mate when I was eventually matched. To *you*."

Olivia blushed, remembering he'd talked about a gift in the cave. He'd kept them here, waiting for her?

"Thank you," she said, taking the box from his hands and perching on the side of the bed with it on her lap. "I'm sure they taste wonderful."

She looked down at the delicious-looking fruits, suddenly having the silly urge to tear up. "I wish I'd brought you something from home… Not that I would've wanted to," she admitted with a laugh. "I thought you were just an alien brute and I was forced into being your match. I didn't want to bring you anything any more than I wanted to come here. But if I'd known just how wrong I was about you, I might've tried to take something with me."

She looked up at him with a smile. Everything had turned out to be so different from what she had thought. But most of all, Kraev had turned out to be different from what she had imagined. She'd thought being matched to a Mahdfel meant the end of her life, but maybe… maybe it wasn't so bad after all?

Kraev looked at her, his turquoise eyes suddenly intense. He sat down beside her and took the box from her hand, setting it on the floor beside them. Olivia frowned, but before she could ask him what he was doing, his lips were already pressed onto hers.

The kiss made her gasp because she hadn't been expecting it. His tail wrapped around her waist and he pulled her close. Her cheeks flushed and her heart leaped in her chest. She wasn't falling for her alien, was she...?

Despite everything, Olivia found herself leaning into the kiss. His lips were soft and gentle. They seemed so at odds with his rough and dangerous image as a warrior, but hadn't he already proven to her that he was more than that?

Heat flooded her as he cradled her face in his hands, turning the kiss from a soft peck to an open-mouthed, passionate one. His tail caressed her sides, leaving a tingling sensation behind. She wrapped her arms around his neck and arched into him, pressing her chest against his still bare one. It was only now that she realized his wounds had pretty much disappeared. He really did have incredible healing powers.

Kraev pulled back just a little, crouching over her with passion flaming in his eyes. "I'm glad you weren't disappointed."

She laughed, tugging him closer again. "You have no idea how glad *I* am that I wasn't disappointed."

Then, she kissed him again.

She hadn't in a million years thought that she would be the one to instigate a kiss with her new alien husband. She'd imagined she was going to have to be forced into being intimate with him at all, that he wouldn't care if she said no.

How wrong she had been.

Now, her body burned under his touch and she couldn't get enough of him.

Realizing she was falling for Kraev opened up a whole new can of worms that she wasn't sure she was mentally ready for. Still, she couldn't stop the feelings. She simply leaned into his embrace, reveling in this moment.

He pushed her back on the bed and Olivia melted into the softness of the sheets. He must have been nearly seven-foot fall and full of muscle, but the bed dwarfed even him. They moved to the middle of the bed where they had all the space in the world to wrap their arms around each other and tangle their legs.

Olivia ran her fingers down Kraev's back, feeling every contour of the hard muscle cultivated there. His tattoos glowed with an intensity she hadn't seen until now, lighting up the entire room. For a moment, she was distracted by the thought of lying there with him and going over what every single one of them meant.

She was too impatient for that right now, though.

It appeared that Kraev was just as impatient. He started trying to undo the buttons on her blouse. His fingers were much thicker than the average human's, and after trying in vain to undo the buttons, he gave in and ripped the blouse open in one button-popping movement.

Olivia couldn't help the giggle that escaped her lips. It was such a cliché move, but somehow, because he was so *different* from how the move was normally envisioned, it didn't seem as cheesy as it should have. She didn't even care to miss her blouse, because it had gotten so dirty in the past days, anyway.

Within seconds, all thoughts of dirty blouses and clichés vanished from her mind though, and the smile left her lips. She lost herself in the feel of his fingers running down her bare neck, over her clothed breasts, and back to the bare skin of her stomach. He kissed the curve of her neck and his tail brushed across her hip. A shiver coursed along her spine.

Not sure what the clothes situation was like on R-2841 yet, Olivia decided it was prudent to remove her own bra rather than let Kraev ruin it when he got frustrated with the even more fiddly clips at the back of it.

She pulled the piece of clothing off slowly, making Kraev pause. He stopped kissing her, his eyes devouring her as the bra fell beside them on the bed, exposing her heavy breasts to the cool air of the room.

He took in a deep breath and said words in a husky tone that the translator couldn't quite catch, moving his lips in a trail down from her neck and toward her breasts.

She gasped when he flicked her nipple with his tongue and then sucked on it gently. A jolt of pleasure went straight to her core and her arm jerked up in what would have been an attempt to lace her fingers through his hair. But his hair didn't really lend itself to having fingers laced through. The shaved sides and intricate braids were too tight. Instead, her hand went automatically to wrap around one of his horns.

He sucked in a sharp breath at the touch, and when she realized what she'd done, she quickly unwrapped her hand. She hadn't realized it might hurt him. She didn't know what the nerves in his horns were like. Stupidly, she hadn't even been thinking about it.

"I'm sor–"

Kraev gave her a heated look, his gaze dark with desire. "You can touch them."

"It doesn't hurt?"

He closed his eyes, taking in a shuddering breath. "No. It feels good."

Olivia's cheeks flushed at the orgasmic expression on his face. Tentatively, she wrapped her hand around his horn again. It felt like it looked: hard and a little ridged. But there was a velvety surface to it too, and as she slid her fingers along it, Kraev let out a guttural moan.

His tail twitched and moved up so that it caressed her left nipple. Then, he leaned down over her right breast. He took it back into his mouth, sucking on the tip and flicking his tongue against it, sending her into a frenzy as his hands roamed her body. Olivia couldn't hold back the moan that escaped her lips.

Her right hand remained on his horn, stroking it, while her left hand ran fingers across his abs and pecs and her legs wrapped around his hips, wanting to get as close as possible. She could feel his hard cock through his pants, and she tightened her grip so that it was pressing into her core.

Kraev grunted against her nipple and thrust into her. His cock brushed against her clit and Olivia gasped. Her entire body felt heated under his touches, and although they'd barely been kissing for five minutes, she already felt like she'd been teased for a lifetime. Just being in his presence for the past two days and not touching him, not kissing him, had led to a level of frustration she'd never felt in her life.

Now that she finally had her hands on him and was allowed to touch him, it was explosive.

She pushed at his pants with her feet, trying to get them around his ankles so that she could pleasure him too. She wanted to press her lips to every inch of his body, but she was equally as unwilling to move to where his tongue wouldn't be swirling around the sensitive nub of her nipple and his hands and tail wouldn't be caressing her.

In the end, her unsuccessful attempts to get his pants off made him pull away from her to remove them anyway. She wanted to pull her own off, but watching him was too arousing. The muscles of his arms and chest bulged as he shimmied his pants off, revealing the powerful legs she'd known would be underneath them.

In the juncture of his thighs, she saw something totally unexpected. His cock was a lighter blue than his skin, nearly the turquoise color of his eyes, but above it, there was a short, two-pronged spur growing out of his skin. It looked like it would press into her clit if he thrust into her at the right angle and she shivered at the prospect.

Her small window of admiration for his gorgeous naked body was cut short when he climbed back on top of her and started pulling at her slacks. Even though he struggled with the clasp, she didn't take over because his fingers were dipping under the top of her panties and coming dangerously close to brushing sensitive areas, and the *almost* factor was driving her wild.

Eventually, he gave up trying to negotiate with the clasp and ripped both that and the zip open anyway. She wiggled her hips while he pulled the pants off and then they were both completely naked.

Breathing hard and skin flushed with desire, she raised herself up on her elbows so she could get another look at his body. The blue skin, horns, and glowing tattoos were something she'd have never thought to find attractive, but seeing him there, his chest rising and falling with barely restrained need was the most erotic thing she'd ever seen in her life.

She kissed him hungrily, crushing their lips together and bringing him back down on top of her. She wrapped her legs around his hips tightly and when his cock slid against her slick entrance, a choked moan escaped them both.

Kraev put one hand on her hip and rested his forehead against hers. His other hand cupped the back of her neck and his tail wrapped around her body.

"My mate," he said softly, his eyes filled with desire, gazing deep into hers as he aligned himself at her entrance.

Olivia gasped as he breached her entrance. He pushed himself into her slowly, stretching her inch by torturous inch. His expression was strained, as if he was scared of hurting her while all he really wanted to do was fuck her senseless.

She wanted that too.

She tightened her legs around his hips again and lifted herself off the bed to take more of him inside her. He groaned in satisfaction and he tightened the grip on her neck, their open mouths brushing against each other but not properly kissing. He was big and she felt completely filled, but she was so slick and wet and turned on that there was no pain.

When he was inside her to the hilt, she felt the advantage of the small, two-pronged spur above his cock. It rubbed against her clit every time he thrust into her, sending her into an entire new world of pleasure that she'd never experienced before. Her breaths were harsh and she moaned with every movement of his hips.

She couldn't get close enough to him, holding him so tightly that she was worried her fingers were bruising him. Her legs were locked in a vice around his hips and she could feel his tail tense up where it began. Her hands moved on his back and it turned her on that he seemed to want her just as much as she wanted him.

He explored her body as if he didn't know where he wanted his hands to be, clinging to her everywhere, from her ass, down her leg, and then back to her hip. He squeezed her tightly, causing just the slightest amount of pleasurable pain.

Their passion built together, getting higher and higher, faster and faster until the coil in her stomach tightened and her climax rushed upon her. She gasped, squeezing her eyes shut even though she wanted to look at him as it became too overwhelming, and let the euphoria roll over her. She felt him climaxing above her, coming hard and deep inside her.

He thrust a few more times into her, his body taut, before collapsing on top of her.

They held each other close, less violently now, and tried to catch their breaths. She still absolutely refused to let go of him and they shifted slightly so that they were lying side by side with her curled around him.

His tail came to wrap around her again and she pressed kisses to his neck and face, and then his lips. This time, it was a long and sensual kiss rather than the heated, desperate ones before.

"*Leani,*" he murmured against her skin.

She glanced up at him. "What does that mean?" It hadn't translated, and she tried to say the word back to him, but it felt foreign on her tongue.

"It's a term of endearment," he said, brushing hair

out of her face and running the same finger all the way down the length of her body, making her shiver. Her skin felt so sensitive. "It's a Raewani word for a life mate. Something akin to beautiful or beloved."

She tried it on her tongue again, just to try and get the sounds right.

A slow, pleased smile spread on Kraev's lips. "Perfect," he said.

Olivia couldn't help but answer with a smile of her own. "I like it," she said. She liked that it didn't translate. It felt unique and special and tied intimately to his culture in a way that it being translated to *sweetheart* or something similar wouldn't have.

"Good, because I will be using it often," he teased.

Olivia giggled. She sunk further into his embrace, feeling the weight of sleep tugging at her eyes. This was the comfiest she'd been... maybe ever, but definitely in the last two days since arriving on R-2841. She wasn't going to be able to stay awake much longer.

Before she succumbed to sleep, she turned to Kraev, looking at him deep in his turquoise eyes. "I'm glad you were my match."

Despite everything, it was undeniably true.

## 14

KRAEV

the next morning, the last thing in the world he wanted to do was get out of bed.

Olivia was wrapped around him, her hand slung over his chest and her face buried in his neck. She was breathing peacefully, seemingly at perfect ease, and it sent a pang of affection through him. He hugged her tighter against him, cradling the back of her head with his hand.

She was so perfect. He had no idea how he could have been so lucky.

The way she had looked when he'd made love to her the night before... He was already hard just thinking about it and his tattoos glowed with a pleasant warmth at the memory. The temptation to wake her up and have another round of passion like that was overwhelming, but he knew he had to resist.

His ultimate duty would always be to his mate, but part of that meant keeping her safe at all times. Right now, that meant adhering to his other duty as a warrior of his clan. There were Suhlik on the surface of the planet, and that threatened not just his mate, but everyone else's too. He knew he had to do everything he could to keep the base safe.

He checked the small computer on his bedside table and saw that the Warlord had called him to a strategic meeting. Since he didn't have a functioning wristband at the moment, he had missed the message and was already a bit late. He prayed the Warlord would grant him a reprieve, since his mate had only just arrived.

Reluctantly, he slipped out of bed, leaving Olivia to wake up alone despite how physically painful doing so was. He dressed quietly, trying his best not to wake her, and kissed her on the forehead before slipping out of the room and into the kitchen. He quickly ate a nourishing, but far too bland, meal from the food replicator and then left his quarters.

Olivia would be able to get out of his quarters without her fingerprint being registered to the system, but she wouldn't be able to get back inside again. He left a note to that effect on the kitchen counter for her.

His trip down to the planet's security headquarters didn't take him long and the Warlord was there waiting for him, talking to another group of warriors. He lifted a hand of acknowledgment to Kraev when he saw him and gestured him over.

"You'll be flying for this team," he said, pulling up a map on his tablet. "You'll be in the next shift, protecting the teleport base. It's our most important asset and we can't afford to lose it. You'll need to fly low to make sure that no stray Suhlik manage to find their way into the building. They've launched another attack in the outer layers of the atmosphere, and I'm worried it's supposed to be a distraction. Your role is crucial here."

Kraev nodded. "Yes, Warlord."

The Warlord held out his hand to Kraev and there was a new wristband in it. "Take this. Zevyk informed me that yours was destroyed in the crash."

"Thank you," he said, taking it and fixing it to his wrist. He would have to get one for Olivia as soon as he got back from this wave of fighting. Then, he would be able to talk to her whenever he wanted, and maybe he wouldn't feel so separated.

He looked around, both at the screens showing the bases that he was fighting to protect and the men that would be fighting with him. The planet was nothing like Raewan, his real home, but wherever Olivia was would be home as far as he was concerned, and he would always be willing to lay his life down to protect that.

And, fighting the Suhlik, laying down your life was always a realistic possibility. He'd learned that lesson from his father. From Zevyk's family.

A knot of something that he couldn't quite place built in his stomach. It was something he'd never felt before, and when he realized what it was, it threw him off guard.

He didn't want to fight.

It was the first time he'd even had a second of doubt about going into battle against the Suhlik, of doing his duty to destroy the evil lizards.

He might die, and that would mean never seeing Olivia again. The thought of that was inconceivable.

But if he died, he would die with the memory of her lips on his, of her body molded perfectly against his. Her soft breaths against his neck as she curled close. That feeling of ultimate peace that had been so intoxicating he'd been sure that it was never going to end, even though that was impossible.

At least they'd had one night together.

A night that might have made Olivia pregnant.

A deep satisfaction at the thought replaced all of

his fears and worries. Maybe his son was starting to grow inside her.

The thought of that warming his heart, new energy filled him. He refused to die today. He would do his everything to come back to Olivia's arms again.

The Suhlik were going down.

# 15

## OLIVIA

OLIVIA EXPECTED to wake up tangled together in bed with her alien husband, warm and comfortable and feeling as content as she had the night before.

Instead, she found herself alone. The large bed was empty, and there was no blue alien in sight. She wrapped her arms around her middle as a shiver ran along her spine. She wasn't actually cold, but she felt chilled somehow without Kraev there beside her.

She took a few more minutes to lie down and look at the rugged rock ceiling of the bedroom before she convinced herself to get out of bed. He might not have even left the apartment. He might still be around, making them breakfast in the kitchen or taking a shower.

She had to admit, the thought of a nice, hot shower was intensely appealing at that moment.

She dragged herself out of bed, finding one of Kraev's shirts in the wardrobe. She pulled it over her head and strode out of the room. She peeked in the living room and the kitchen, but to her disappointment, she couldn't find Kraev anywhere in the apartment.

He must have gone scouting already, like he'd said last night…

She explored the quarters on her own, finally opening the two other doors that she hadn't investigated the day before. One of them was the bathroom and she almost swooned at the sight of the bath. Well, bath or hot tub, she couldn't quite decide.

Either way, she started pressing buttons on the control panel – whose bath had a control panel, anyway? – until it started to fill with water at the perfect temperature. She pulled the shirt over her head and sank into the bath. One of the buttons turned on jets and she sighed in pleasure.

She was too antsy to really enjoy the bath, though. Within ten minutes, she'd given her body a quick scrub, washed her hair, and let the water go, feeling a bit bad for wasting it.

The final door led to a small closet-like room, filled with boxes and storage. The main centerpiece of the room was a machine that reminded her of the food replicator on a larger scale. It wasn't huge, but it came up to her waist. The screen was like the food replicator's, too, and she realized pretty quickly what it did.

It seemed like some far superior 3D printer. Pictures of different kinds of items showed on the screen. Clothes, household items, and miscellaneous things she couldn't even begin to name…

Could it actually make all these things? Excited, Olivia clicked on some basic clothes, quickly finding a small selection of Earth models. The machine started buzzing, and soon, a blue T-shirt appeared in the box. It was soft and nearly indistinguishable from something she might have bought in the store.

She stared at it in awe, feeling the fabric under her fingers. How did this thing work? It really seemed to be able to replicate matter to make whatever she wanted. The selection wasn't big, but she clicked on a few more items on the screen. A pair of jeans, a sweater, and sneakers, and she was good to go.

She hurried into them and returned to the kitchen. Her stomach was rumbling, but with the food replicator, she could make herself something quickly. She nearly laughed at the idea because it no longer seemed so foreign to her. Machines seemed to make everything here. Hadn't Kraev said they also did the mining on the planet?

She went for a simple bagel and cream cheese. Again, it had the strange artificial taste, but she thought she'd probably get used to that pretty quickly, especially if most of the things she ate came from it. Though Kraev seemed to prefer *real* food rather than this created stuff, so maybe they would be having proper breakfasts more often.

It was hard to imagine what their life was going to look like. Nothing had been straightforward or normal since her arrival on R-2841. Even now, there was still an immediate threat from the Suhlik. If the Suhlik threat was ever gone, if it calmed down for a while, how would they spend their days?

Right now, all she hoped was that they'd be spending a lot of them in bed together. She ached in the best way possible and would have killed to have him there in front of her, as naked as he'd been the night before.

She sighed. On the kitchen table, she found a note letting her know what she had already suspected: Kraev had gone scouting. The note also explained the fingerprint entry system to Kraev's quarters, and that she wouldn't be able to return if she left.

Still, Olivia didn't want to stay in his quarters all alone. She was sure that there'd be someone outside that she could ask to fix the fingerprint issue for her, even if most of the base were out searching for the hiding lizards.

Finishing off the last of her bagel, she left the apartment.

It felt strange walking around without her phone, wallet, and keys, but she'd brought none of them with her to R-2841 and wouldn't have had any use for them either. She kept patting her pockets and feeling a shred of panic that she'd left them at home, though. She wondered how long that would last.

She started walking back toward the rings, wondering if she'd be able to find Kraev, or if he'd have left on his scouting mission already. She didn't think he'd have left the bed unless he was required to at that specific moment, but it didn't stop her hoping.

Scouting didn't sound especially dangerous, but the thought of him out there with the Suhlik still made her heart thump in her chest.

"Can I help you?"

A woman's voice made her jump and turn around. She hadn't realized how slowly she'd been walking, completely lost in her own thoughts, until the woman had stopped her.

She looked like Kraev, insofar as her skin was a deep blue hue and her hair, though not shaved, was braided in the same intricate way as the other

Raewani descendants she'd seen. She wore a colorful, embroidered dress and large jewel earrings. She must have been from his home planet, which, being a female, made her a full-blooded Raewani.

The woman had a baby in her arms that was sleeping soundly, and Olivia felt a tug in her gut upon seeing the tiny infant and its screwed up but still peaceful face.

"Hi," Olivia said. "Sorry, I'm just kind of wandering aimlessly. It's my first day on the base, and I don't really know where anything is."

"I'm Naia," the woman said. "I can show you around, if you'd like. I've lived here for several years now."

"That would be amazing." Olivia smiled. "Thank you. I'm Olivia, by the way."

The woman nodded. "The mate of Kraev from Tayn. I have already heard the rumors of your arrival."

Olivia cocked an eyebrow at the woman. "Rumors?"

The woman smiled slightly, cradling the baby in her arms. "Not so much rumors, perhaps. This is but a small base. Word travels fast and you are the first Earthling on the planet. There has been talk."

"The first– I'm the only human here?" Olivia's brows shot up at the news. Somehow, she hadn't really considered the fact. All of the warriors she'd seen so far were the blue-skinned Raewan-Mahdfel, but she hadn't considered that there might be *only* Raewani descendants on this planet.

"Yes. There are some warriors and mates who are not from Raewan, but mostly this planet is populated by those blessed by Rae."

"Rae?" Somehow, the woman spoke in an enigmatic manner, unlike Kraev. It made Olivia wonder whether she and Kraev were even speaking the same language to her. Maybe Kraev spoke a Mahdfel language and the woman spoke whatever her people spoke on Raewan. Or maybe it was just a different dialect and the translator was picking up on that.

"The star that gives light to our planet," Naia explained, starting to lead her toward the rings in the center of the base. Again, it was eerily silent in the hallways.

"Is it normally busier here?" Olivia asked, peering over the edge of one of the rings and looking at the vast expanse of the cavern around her. It was such a huge space. "Or is it just really underpopulated?"

"It is normally much busier. When the Suhlik are gone, the rings bustle with life. It is strange for me to see it this quiet, too. I should be in my quarters, really, but Mito over here doesn't like being cooped up. It makes him antsy. He'd been crying for hours, so I thought I'd just take him for a walk. He calmed down and fell asleep almost immediately."

She pushed the hair out of the infant's face and curled her finger over his cheek, looking at him with the pure affection that Olivia imagined was reserved for parent and child.

She felt the silly urge to put her hand over her stomach. There was a chance she was pregnant, wasn't there? They hadn't used protection last night. Her own tiny blue baby might be growing in her stomach at that very moment.

"He's beautiful," she said to Naia. "I can't imagine that angelic face crying at all."

Naia laughed, her earrings jingling. "Trust me, he is very good at it. You've caught him at an opportune moment. I just hope that the battle does not get too close to the base. That would definitely set him off again. I do not wish to have to hole up in my quarters if I can help it."

"Battle?" Olivia asked, her gut-wrenching. "I thought they were just out scouting for any remaining Suhlik."

"No." Naia shook her head, a slight frown forming between her brows. "There was another attack on the outer atmosphere this morning. Suhlik ships are pouring in toward the planet. It's all hands on deck that can fight." She turned to Olivia. "You didn't know this?"

"Kraev didn't say anything." The wave of panic that hit her was overwhelming. A full-scale attack? And Kraev was out there, fighting on the front lines? "Last night, he said that he'd be gone scouting this morning, so I just assumed…"

"The attack came this morning. He probably didn't know it then. Or he didn't want you to worry."

"I'll always worry!" she said, surprised by the vehemence in her voice, but knowing that it was true. How had her emotions reached this point so quickly? "Do you know where they'll be? Do you think he'll have flown out yet?"

Naia lifted a single shoulder in a small shrug that didn't disturb Mito. "I have no knowledge of such. Depending on when his shift is, it is possible that they're still preparing the ship for moving out."

With her heart in her throat, she turned to start the run toward the hangar, praying that she could remember where it actually was. "Thank you!" she said to Naia over her shoulder, keeping her voice low so she didn't wake the baby. "Hopefully, I'll see you again. It was nice to meet you."

She didn't wait to hear a response, and sprinted toward the elevator. Her footfalls echoed loudly in the deserted corridor, but she barely heard them.

She pressed the elevator call button a dozen times before it opened and she hurried in, trusting her gut on which floor the hangar had been on.

There, she raced through empty corridors toward the hangar and started to see more warriors heading in the same direction. Some of them gave her curious looks, but no one actually stopped her.

When she was almost at the door, she spotted the back of a head she already knew like the back of her hand. She would have been able to recognize the intricate braiding of his hair, the distinct color of his skin, and the sway of his tail anywhere.

"Kraev!" she shouted.

He immediately turned to her, his eyes wide and surprised to see her. The team he was with stopped too, and he gestured without looking back for them to go ahead.

He opened his arms and she ran into them, not able to slow her pace quite enough as she got to him, crushing herself against his hard chest. His tail wrapped around her body and she immediately flung her arms around his back. She buried her face in his leather armor, taking in the scent that was all Kraev.

Trying to catch her breath, she attempted to sort out the jumbled thoughts in her head.

"You're going to fight," she said simply, trying not to make it sound like an accusation.

"I am." He tucked her hair behind her ears. "I didn't want to worry you. I didn't know that there was a full-scale attack happening until I met with the Warlord this morning. By that point, there was no way to contact you, except to leave a message on the computer at my quarters and I didn't think that would have been fair."

It was on the tip of her tongue to argue with him, to say that she always wanted to know if he was about to do something as dangerous as this, but the words didn't come.

"I'm scared," she said instead.

"I'm scared too," he admitted, and it was surprising coming from his mouth. She didn't think he'd looked scared once while they'd been fighting. He was so powerful, so strong, that she couldn't imagine him being scared of anything.

He pushed another lock of hair back from her face, looking deep into her eyes. His turquoise eyes had a distinct darkness to them, and she could see that he was terrified of not coming back to her.

"You have to come back to me," she said, answering those fears with words. "You have to."

Kraev smiled at her gently. "I'll do everything in my power to get back to you," he said, resting his forehead against hers. It wasn't the promise she'd wanted to hear and he seemed to realize that, even if she was trying not to show it on her face. "I promise I'll come back to you. Soon, I'll be right here, holding you just like this."

She was under no illusions. She knew that it was a promise that he couldn't actually give, but it still made her feel infinitely better.

She stood on her tiptoes, cupping his face with her hands. She hesitated before kissing him, taking in every inch of his perfect face and his eyes which held nothing back. All his love was right there in his expression. He wasn't ashamed or abashed by it, and it took her breath away.

He did have to come back.

She had no idea what she'd do if he didn't come back to her.

She kissed him tenderly, barely brushing her lips against his at first. She had to stand on her toes and crane her neck to even kiss him, and she wished they were back on his bed, where she could wrap herself around him more easily.

He deepened the kiss, opening his mouth and asking her to meet the movement. Their tongues entangled and their bodies moved as close together as it was possible to be.

She knew it was completely inappropriate, but

she couldn't stop the coil of desire that tightened in her stomach, or the heat that pooled between her thighs. If he hadn't been about to fight for his life, she would have dragged him to the nearest secluded space and had a repeat of their night together.

But eventually, they had to pull back. She tucked her face into his neck and held him tightly.

"Be safe," she said softly, not sure if he'd even be able to hear her above the sounds of the hangar just behind them.

"I'll be safe," he promised. "And you stay safe, too. Stay in the residential areas, near my quarters. They'll be safest if something does go wrong. I'll ask someone to get your fingerprints added to my quarters so that you can come and go as you please. Everyone here will know who you are, as you're the only human on the base. It won't be any problem."

Talking about these logistics was the last thing she wanted to do. Now was when she should have been making outpourings of love, but the words stuck in her throat. Everything had been so sudden. She still hadn't quite reconciled it with herself. She couldn't bring herself to say those things, even though she knew she might never get another chance.

"Tell me as soon as you're back," she said instead. "I don't know how you'll get in touch with me, but you have to promise that you'll tell me as soon as you're back."

"Of course, *leani*," he murmured, kissing her once more, then pulling away before she could deepen the kiss. He was about to move away, but then came back again and peppered kisses all over her face. "I'll be back."

Then, he was gone, striding away from her and not turning back. He passed through the double doors of the hangar and they shut behind him.

For a moment, Olivia stood rooted to the floor, unable to turn away from where he'd been moments ago.

She jumped violently when someone lay a hand on her shoulder, and turned to see she'd been surprised by Naia again.

"Oh," she said, calming her breathing. "Sorry, you gave me a fright."

Naia must have followed her down from the residential area to make sure she was okay, or perhaps to see if her own mate hadn't left yet. Mito was still sleeping soundly on her arm.

"It's hard," Naia said, turning away from the door and making it easier for Olivia to follow suit. "Watching them go out when you don't know if they'll ever come back. It's also something you have to learn to accept, unfortunately."

Olivia sighed, her gaze focused on the small blue face of Mito, who was sleeping so peacefully despite all the danger his father must currently have been in.

"Is it like this often?" she asked. "I don't know… raising a family on a planet where this happens often, I don't know if I'd be able to do it."

"It isn't usually this bad, but the attacks have been getting worse lately," Naia admitted. "Hopefully, we'll deal a big blow in this fight and the Suhlik will realize that it isn't worth it to keep throwing resources at us when we always manage to fight back."

Olivia's hand rested on her stomach for half a second as they started to make their way back through the corridors and up toward the sixth floor of the rings.

"I was so against it when I first was matched," she admitted quietly. "And then, the second I teleported here, I was almost killed by a Suhlik. Everything was so wildly different. I'm just here to make babies, and when I'm finally coming around to the possibility, my match is sent off to fight for his life. What's the point in me being here if I can't even have children because he's out fighting?"

"It is the way of the Mahdfel," Naia said just as quietly. "If Kraev dies and you're not pregnant, you'll be sent back to Earth to live the life you had before."

Surprisingly, panic rose in her chest rather than relief.

Being sent back to Earth.

Kraev being dead.

"What if I was pregnant?" It was a possibility. She couldn't rule it out.

"Then the Mahdfel clan here would take care of you and the child. You'll always be a part of our family."

Olivia shook her head. "No. That's not right," she said. "None of that would be right. Kraev can't die. Kraev could never be dead." She couldn't even bear to think about him not returning right now, whether she was pregnant or not. Even the thought of picking up back on Earth where she'd left off wasn't the balm she'd expected it to be.

Going back to medical school, completing her degree and becoming a doctor. Seeing her family again.

None of it would be the same because she'd known Kraev and then lost him.

She had the urge to sprint back down to the hangar, to see again if he'd departed yet and to beg him desperately to stay. It would have been wholly unfair and she would have forced him to deny her, but if he'd been in front of her right then, she wouldn't have been able to stop herself.

Naia rested a hand on her arm. "Everything will work out," she promised. "Fate always knows what it is doing, even if it doesn't seem like it at the time."

It definitely didn't seem like fate had her best interests at heart right now. If it had, she would have been curled up in bed with Kraev, having just woken up and about to have another round of the incredible sex they'd shared the night before.

Instead, she was walking through the empty halls of a place she couldn't quite call home yet, feeling sick with anxiety.

"I'm going to just keep wandering around the place," Olivia said, not able to find the strength to be positive for Naia right now. "I think I'd rather be on my own, if you don't mind. I just want to think things through."

"Of course." Naia gave her the location of her quarters so that Olivia would be able to find her again if she needed any help with anything, and then headed off with Mito on her arm.

Olivia took a long breath in and sighed deeply.

Her head was spinning with the implications of everything that was happening right now and she just wanted some peace.

Kraev being home and safe would have given her all the peace she was craving, but clearly, it wasn't meant to be right now.

## 16

___

## KRAEV

IT TOOK ALL the willpower Kraev possessed to not turn around as he walked toward the hangar. Every muscle in his body begged him to look over his shoulder and catch Olivia's gaze again, to turn around and bundle her back into his arms, wrap his tail tightly around her, and never let go.

But he couldn't.

He knew that he couldn't.

With every second that he spent here on the surface, not in his ship, he was letting the Suhlik get closer and closer.

Letting them get closer to harming Olivia.

He couldn't allow that to happen.

So, he stepped through the doors and continued on to where the ship he'd be piloting was waiting in the hangar for him.

The nagging urge in his mind to turn back didn't let up, though. Not even when he stepped inside the body of the medium-sized fighter. It was just like the one that Zevyk had arrived on for the mountain rescue. Kraev had piloted this specific ship many times in the past.

He was surprised, as he headed toward the bridge, to see Zevyk in the corridor, doing something with the wiring behind a wall panel.

"You're on the team, too?" he asked.

"Yes," Zevyk replied. "I wasn't at the briefing because the ship still needed work, but it's nearly finished. Issues with the comms system. It was broken at different parts of the ship. Non-essential, but if I need to fix something else, it would be good if I could speak to you properly."

When Kraev only grunted his acknowledgment, Zevyk glanced up at him. "What's wrong?"

"I shouldn't be here," he admitted, though it felt wrong to even say the words out loud.

"I know you feel bad about not having been able to fight properly in the initial attack, but this is the time you make up for that. We'll be up in the skies soon. I'm working as fast as I can." Zevyk turned back to his wires and did just that, as if to make the point.

Kraev shook his head and almost wanted to

laugh. Before he met Olivia, he would have made the same assumptions that Zevyk just had, that his only reason for being upset was that he *wasn't* fighting, that he felt like he was letting his clan down by having not been on the front line of the previous fight.

But no, he felt like he was letting them down for an altogether different reason.

"That's not what I meant," Kraev said. "I mean here, fighting at all. My mate is here on the base. She's worried about me, and I'm worried about her. I've barely known her for any time at all. What if I never come back to her? Or what if something happens to her and I'm not here to help?"

He rubbed the back of his neck as he spoke, almost ashamed to admit it. He was a warrior. Fighting to protect the clan should always be something that he wanted to do. But he trusted Zevyk more than anyone. He knew that his brother would at least try to understand, even if he couldn't.

"She's safe here inside the volcano," Zevyk said. "And going out there is how you keep her safe. You're one of the best pilots on the planet. You being out there is the best chance you have of making sure that nothing ever happens to hurt her."

"I know." He shook his head. "Rationally, I know,

but in here–" He put his hand over his heart. "It's tearing me apart to be away from her."

Zevyk turned away from the panel he was working on and rested his hands on Kraev's arms. "This is new for you and it's intense. I know it's the worst possible timing, but you *are* doing the best thing for her. You must know that deep down, too."

Kraev nodded, though his heart felt like it might split. He did know that. And honestly, he didn't even *want* to shirk his duty. He was a warrior. Mahdfel. He would always fight the Suhlik, to the death if that was what it came to. But finding his mate had shaken up his priorities in a way he hadn't been expecting, making him feel things he hadn't before and ask questions he'd never even considered until this day.

They'd all lost people to the Suhlik. They all knew how dangerous and unpredictable the lizards could be. But keeping Olivia – keeping his family – safe was his first priority as a warrior. He *couldn't* shirk his duties.

He thought back to the Suhlik and the atrocities they had committed. His blood immediately started to boil in anger and he let his instincts take control. He had a good sense for battle and he was good at trusting his instincts when it came to deciding whether to attack or retreat, whether he should be in a ship or on the ground.

"You're right," he finally said. "Get back to fixing the problem so that we can get flying as soon as possible. I want these scum out of our atmosphere and sent back with a message that they shouldn't bother trying to attack us again."

Zevyk smiled. "I have no doubt that the bastards will be too terrified to even think of coming back to the planet after what we're about to do to them."

Kraev grinned back at him and tried to let the thrill of the fight fuel him like he always had in the past. It worked, to a certain extent. He wasn't as fired up as he usually was, but hopefully, the feeling would come when they took off.

He walked up to the bridge where the rest of his crew were already strapped in and running programs on their screens to make sure that everything was ready for lift-off.

He sank into the captain's chair and started playing around with his own screen, making sure the ship's diagnostics were all showing green lights. There was a single amber warning on the comms system, but that was what Zevyk was fixing as they spoke. Everything else was good to go.

The earlier shift had not yet ended, but the

sooner they could provide assistance to the teleport base, the better. The Suhlik could all go to hell.

"We're going to be flying fast and low," Kraev said. "It's going to be a bumpy ride."

"We're all strapped in and ready to go," the weapons guy, Delyn, replied. "Weapons systems are all up and running and ready to fire at will."

"Glad to hear it," Kraev said. Having someone else actually operating the weapons systems rather than trying to do his best with them while also flying was going to make everything a thousand times easier than it had been during his and Olivia's escape. On this size ship, he needed a full crew to make it run effectively.

And as much as he missed her already, not having Olivia actually on the ship was a massive advantage.

He was sure that he'd zone into the fight eventually, and when that happened, not having his mate anywhere near him would mean he could do whatever needed to be done without risking hurting her. He knew what his crew's limits were because they were all Mahdfel. Flying with a human on the ship had made him second-guess what he could push for.

The light on his screen changed from amber to green and then Zevyk's voice echoed through the bridge. "Comms are good to go. Ready for take-off. I'm going to strap in in the engineering bay."

Kraev started flicking the switches that would bring the ship to life. It was a good warship, ready for a fight in the atmosphere but would have struggled if forced into the vacuum of space for any length of time. It was perfect for the type of fight he was about to dive headfirst into.

Thrusters roared to life and he flexed his fingers on the controls.

He didn't think about Olivia. He pushed her as far to the back of his mind as was possible for someone he cared so intensely about, and tried to sink into the immediate situation. Suhlik. Flying. Fighting. Winning.

"Strapped in?" he asked Zevyk.

"Strapped in and ready."

Kraev urged the joystick forward and the ship lifted off.

# 17

## OLIVIA

OLIVIA DIDN'T WANT to go back to the apartment – not that she was even sure she could. Kraev had said that he would get someone to add her fingerprints to the locking system, but she didn't know if that meant she had to go and find someone to *give* her fingerprints or not.

So, she wandered aimlessly around the base for a while, hoping that she would be able to push images of Kraev's mangled body after a shipwreck out of her mind. They had survived a shipwreck just days ago, right? He could survive another one if it came to that.

Part of her was still so overwhelmed by the engineering feat and the many tunnels that formed the volcano base that she almost did manage to forget about how much danger her mate was in, even if only for a second.

When had she started thinking of him as her mate?

It was a term she hadn't even really heard before until now, outside of maybe biology class, but she could tell from the way he used it that it was a very serious thing in Mahdfel culture. She would have to ask him about it, but it seemed that he very much meant it in the traditional sense: a mate for life.

That meant more than just telling someone you loved them – which she still hadn't done either – or even being married to someone. People who were married could always get a divorce if they wanted to. If you were *mated* that meant more than that. You couldn't unmate with someone, could you?

She wandered through warmly lit metal corridors and knew that she was getting lost. There was no one around and, after a while, all of the corridors started to look the same. There were no signposts or maps anywhere. She didn't even have a way to contact anyone. She didn't have one of the fancy wristbands that all the other occupants of the base seemed to wear.

She had no desire to be found for a little bit longer either, though. She was happy to walk along faceless corridors with nothing but her thoughts.

Wallowing was easy.

After a while, she walked past an open door. It was the first that she'd come to since starting her stroll. It was only when she noticed the open door that she realized the corridors had changed slightly, too. They were wider here, and the doors seemed larger and further apart than when she'd been walking through the residential area.

Not wanting to disturb anyone, she peered through the open doorway from a distance.

Inside were a group of young boys who must not have been older than seven or eight. One of the boys was holding a spear and executing a series of complicated movements with it. Initially, she was impressed. He was graceful and powerful for such a young kid, and seemed like he knew exactly what he was doing with the weapon.

Then, he broke out of the impressive movements and sprinted toward a dummy, impaling it through the chest with his spear.

Olivia's heart sank.

If she was pregnant, was that her son's future? Spending time in the gym since he was just a kid, learning how to kill as soon as he was old enough to learn to walk?

Would she end up being left alone at home, worrying about not just Kraev, but her sons, too?

She was sure she remembered Kraev saying that all Mahdfel boys received warrior training from a young age. She knew that it was a part of their culture, that it was important to them, but the thought of her sons living that life didn't exactly fill her with joy.

The boy inside the training room grabbed his spear and started doing the movements again. The other children took up spears and followed him. It was silly, but it was only now that Olivia realized that they were practicing fighting formations and not just doing some kind of dance or gymnastics routine.

She was too innocent for this planet, even after all the horror she'd seen in her childhood.

She didn't want to think about any of it.

Turning away from the door without speaking to the children, she caught a flash of blue at the other end of the corridor before it disappeared. Frowning, she walked back and saw Naia. She was leaning against the corridor's wall, pushing the hair out of Mito's eyes.

"Hello," Naia said, an impish smile on her face.

Olivia frowned. "Are you following me?"

The woman gave her an inscrutable look. "Maybe."

Olivia didn't know how to react to that. She'd at least expected a denial. "Why?"

"Because you've only just arrived on the planet and already your mate has gone off to battle. I know that this must be a difficult time for you. I just wanted to be there to make sure I could step in if it got to be too much for a moment," she replied, lifting one shoulder in an elegant shrug. "I hope I have not offended you."

Olivia blinked in surprise. "Not at all," she said.

If anything, it almost made her tear up. It was so sweet. A slight part of her anxiety was because she didn't know a single person on the base. She was apparently the only human here and she felt alone. But now, that feeling lessened, even if just a bit.

She smiled at Naia. "Thank you. For caring. That means a lot."

Talking to Naia might even distract her a little bit. She'd asked to spend time on her own because she was worried about burdening the woman with her thoughts, but Naia didn't seem burdened at all.

The woman smiled back at her, a part of her own hesitancy seeming to disappear. "Of course. We are part of the same clan now. Of course, I care."

Her words were more reassuring than Olivia could've ever imagined. Tears did spring to her eyes now, but she pushed them back.

Naia gestured for Olivia to follow her and they returned to the door that she'd been peering through. "That's my son," she said, gesturing to the same boy Olivia had been watching before. He was still practicing the fighting maneuvers with the other children. "Feishik, though we call him Fei."

Olivia wasn't sure how to respond to that. She didn't want to admit that she'd been thinking it was wrong to be learning to fight so young, so she simply said, "He looks very talented."

Naia nodded, looking pleased. "He is. His father has taught him well. Fei has always wanted to be exactly like his father. He is very skilled with the *astav* spear."

Hearing their voices in the doorway, Fei turned and spotted his mother and Olivia. He raised the hand with his spear as a greeting and then started performing even more complicated moves. It culminated in him landing incorrectly and falling on his ass. His light blue cheeks turned purple, and Olivia realized she hadn't known the Mahdfel could blush.

She chuckled, though she tried to hide it with a cough.

Naia was laughing too. "Just keep practicing, my son," she said. "We'll leave you to do it in private.

Make sure you let me know when you're ready to leave the training room."

"Yes, Mom," he replied, turning his back on them so that they couldn't see his embarrassed face.

They walked outside and Naia said, "Just like his father. He was always trying to impress me and making a fool of himself, too." The words were said with an affectionate smile.

"Is he out fighting?" Olivia asked, worried that the question would bring the mood down.

"He is. There are always some warriors who stay behind at the base to defend it and my mate is often among them. But today, he is out fighting with the fleet at the teleport base."

"Are you worried?"

"Of course. The worry never goes away when we are apart, but you get better at handling it, I promise. Having Fei and Mito here helps, too. They're being good today, but normally they're so much of a handful when their father goes to fight that I don't have time to think about anything else anyway." She cradled the baby affectionately to her chest. "I wouldn't change a single part of it."

Olivia's fingers brushed against her stomach for the hundredth time that day. Every time she did, she became more and more excited by the idea that maybe she was pregnant. She could imagine her and

Naia together, each of them nursing their own babies and talking as they did now about everything under the sun.

"Are Fei and Mito your only children?" she asked. It was hard to get a grip on the age of the Raewani people, but she didn't think Naia looked very old.

"For now, yes. Though I'm certain that another child will come soon." She rested her hand on her own stomach. "I'm going to be blessed with a large family, I know it."

"Kraev wants a large family," Olivia said, unsure why she was telling this woman all her hopes and fears, as if they'd been best friends for years. "He comes from a huge family back on Raewan, but my family was small. Just my parents, me, and my brother. I don't know if I'd be able to handle that many kids."

"It wouldn't be *you* handling it. It would be both of you handling it together, and the rest of the clan to help you when you need it."

Olivia wasn't sure why she continued to be surprised by these things. Her father had always been good to her and very involved in raising her. He'd taught her how to ride a bicycle and later, after the Suhlik had invaded, how to shoot a gun. She wasn't at all in disbelief that a man could raise a child, but once again, her prejudices about the Mahdfel were preceding her.

Kraev had already proven that it was nothing like how she'd always expected. She was allowed to work. She was respected and even worshiped by him. It wasn't unreasonable to think that he would want to take just as active a role in parenting as hers.

Somehow, the thought still came as a bit of a shock. She had never pictured a big, hulky warrior in a fatherly role. But Naia was right. It wouldn't just be her surrounded by a horde of children, it would be her and her mate surrounded by a horde of children that they loved more than anything in the world.

She put her fingers to her stomach again and was even more excited than the last time she'd thought about the possibility of a boy growing inside her.

"You're right," she said to Naia. "Sorry, I'm having a bit of culture shock, still."

"It's only been a few turns of the world since you arrived," Naia said. "Of course, things haven't fully sunk in yet." She looked at the corridor they were in. "Would you like me to show you around the base, properly this time?"

Olivia smiled. "That would be great. Thank you."

"It is my pleasure." Naia returned the smile and they started walking.

Olivia told her about what she'd actually known about Mahdfel before she'd been sent here, admitting that it was barely anything. Barbaric warriors and baby making.

Naia laughed. "It was much the same for me. I'm from a small, secluded tribe on Raewan. We have quite the opposite outlook on the Mahdfel. We revere them as almost gods. Raewan cities are quite modern, but in the tribal regions, we still live by the old ways. We barely had any technology and all that we did have came from the Mahdfel. Most of it was specifically so that we could identify matches for the Mahdfel and then get in touch with them afterward. In the tribes, we have a yearly coming of age ceremony for the girls and then a matching ceremony straight afterward."

"That's so strange," Olivia admitted. "Everyone is tested immediately as they come of age?"

"Yes. The way of the testing may differ from planet to planet, but it happens much the same way everywhere in the universe. It's the only way the Mahdfel can survive and they've helped many cultures survive too. It's a system that benefits everyone. It just doesn't take into account the emotional impact."

Olivia looked at the woman in surprise. "You didn't want to be a match?"

Naia lifted a shoulder. "It was tough for me. If I had not been a match then, I would have had to marry my tribe leader's son, and I didn't want to do that. But I also didn't want to leave Raewan and my family behind. In the end, I regret nothing. But at the time, I was so scared of leaving my family and moving to a whole new planet. I was torn."

Olivia nodded empathetically. "That's exactly how I feel. At first, I was so against this. I didn't want to leave my family and my career, but now that I've met Kraev, I can't say that I could just go back to Earth anymore either. As crazy as it sounds, considering we've only known each other for a few days, I don't think I could live without him. I'm torn, too."

Naia nodded. "It gets easier. You settle in and you start to adjust. Especially when you have children, you realize that all that matters is that you have your family close."

"I know you're right," she said, sighing. "It's just hard to look that far ahead when so many overwhelming things are happening right now."

"I understand. There will probably be a lull after this fight and then you can settle into the routine of living here more normally. Are you hungry?" she asked suddenly. "We have places we can eat in our quarters of course, but there's plenty of communal eating areas too. Sometimes, it's nice to go and eat with other people, and the chefs are amazing."

"Do you have like… currency here?" Olivia asked, feeling silly as she did.

Naia shook her head. "No, nothing like that. Things are provided for people as they're needed. A certain amount of privilege comes with status, but there is no one who goes without."

Olivia found that she liked this idea, that people would always be provided for. Working in the hospital, she'd seen too many people coming through who she'd been unable to help the way they wanted because of financial constraints.

That probably meant that, if she did continue her medical training here, she would be able to help everyone equally. She wouldn't have to consider funding or insurance. She could always work to make sure everyone was okay. The thought of that spread a happy warmth through her.

The canteen that they headed to was in the middle of the volcano. It was a large, dome-shaped room with a food counter in the middle and tables in rings extending out from it. There was no one behind the counter serving the food; it was more of an *all-you-can-eat* style buffet than anything else.

She tried not to look too excited as they walked toward it. There were a few stragglers in the canteen, but no one paid them any mind. A couple of women with their sons, and a couple more women sat in a group, chatting and eating. They were all Raewani and two of them were heavily pregnant.

"Is this all from the food replicators?" Olivia asked as they looked at what was on offer.

"Not all of it," Naia replied, handing her a plate and trying to put things on her own while still holding the sleeping Mito.

"Let me help you," Olivia said. "Just tell me what you want me to dish up."

Naia smiled. "Thank you. The fruit is all from the greenhouses outside."

She gestured to two large bowls filled with blue-tinged fruit. Some of them looked like the candied fruits that Kraev had gotten Olivia from Raewan, and the thought almost jolted her back into the anxious mess that she was. She had been trying to avoid thinking about him too much. What if he died and she had never tried the gift he'd given her? She had meant to try them the night before, but he'd immediately distracted her by taking her to bed.

"The meat products are mostly from the food replicators," Naia continued, either not realizing Olivia was distracted, or trying to drag her thoughts back to the present. "And most of the mixed dishes. Sometimes, people will cook dishes from the fruit and vegetables we can grow on the planet, but when a fight like this happens, almost everything is from a replicator because it's quicker."

She gestured to a line of devices that Olivia recognized. "They have bigger replicators here too, if you want to create your own food. I know it must be strange coming to somewhere new with an entirely new diet."

Olivia had never been fussy about food and the thought of trying something different was actually intriguing. The whole universe was at her fingertips with the replicators, too.

She selected some meat in a red sauce that smelled like it was going to be quite sweet, and some vegetables. Onto Naia's plate, she placed some fresh fruit and a slab of what appeared to be a sort of pie.

They sat at a nearby table and Naia ate one-handed while Olivia shoveled food into her mouth with a three-pronged fork.

"How come they put food out if they've got replicators as well?" she asked. Surely, it made more sense for them to just let everyone replicate their own food, unless it was fresh. Then they could have exactly what they wanted.

"When there isn't a battle happening, it can get very busy here at mealtimes," Naia said. "People will come here to eat as a family and it's quicker to get things from the buffet than to queue up for the replicators."

"That makes sense."

"Cooking is also a cultural thing for many people. Many of the women here come from places without food replicators, like me. I cook in the kitchens here sometimes. There are many old recipes from my village that are close to my heart. It makes me feel closer to my heritage to cook even if I replicate the ingredients that I make the meal with." She lifted a shoulder. "It sounds kind of silly, I know, but I like sharing my culture that way."

Olivia nodded eagerly. "That does sound good," she said. "If I'm the only person from Earth here, maybe that's something I could do too, share with people food that they've never tried before."

She liked to cook, although she wasn't great at it by any means. But it might make her feel closer to the rest of the people on the planet too, to make it feel more like home if she gave back instead of just taking.

"I'd love to try something from Earth," Naia said. "I don't really know anything about the planet."

Olivia smiled. "It's a deal then. I'll make you some Earth food."

They continued to eat and chatted about their respective cultures and previous homes. Halfway through dinner, Mito woke up, but he was in a cheery mood and gurgled happily as they fussed him.

"Do you want to hold him?" Naia asked.

Olivia only hesitated for a second, and then accepted the happy baby into her arms. She cradled him how she'd seen Naia holding him, and cooed at him as she had been doing. He immediately grabbed her finger and began to gnaw on it with his gums.

"Sorry," Naia apologized, going to remove the hand for her. "His teeth are coming through."

"It's fine, I'll stop him if it hurts," she said, smiling.

The baby felt so right in her arms. She wished that Kraev was there behind her, holding her close and looking just as excitedly at the infant, more than ready to have their own baby in their arms. She had never much considered being a mother before. With her studies, it hadn't been a prevalent topic in her life. But now, she wondered if she could somehow combine her studies and motherhood.

"He's perfect," Olivia said.

Naia laughed, looking like she was about to make a comment about how he could be a nightmare some of the time, but then her face softened. "Yeah, he really is perfect."

Olivia completely ignored her food to keep

playing with the baby in her arms. A strange warmth filled her as she did so. She couldn't remember the last time she'd held one, maybe it was never. All that she could think about now was how excited it made her to hold her own baby. Her and Kraev's baby.

She just couldn't wait for him to be home.

## 18

### KRAEV

THE FLIGHT to the teleport base wasn't long. They kept the two places at a fair distance for this exact reason. If there was an attack, the main target would almost always be the teleport base. From the teleport base, the Suhlik could immediately bring in massive reinforcements that would allow them to turn the tides on a battle.

It would also prevent the Mahdfel defending the base from doing the exact same thing. Unlike the Suhlik, the Mahdfel were stretched more thinly across the universe and so they would only call in reinforcements if they absolutely had to. It hadn't reached that point on R-2841 yet.

But there was a reason why the base wasn't right by the volcano, either. It couldn't be, because the volcano was filled with hellstone that prevented teleportation, but it was also a strategic choice. If the Suhlik were at the teleport base, it meant they weren't close enough to the volcano base to get to the mines or cause any collateral damage. It meant the women and children would always be as safe as they could be.

The teleport base, however, was not safe at all. There were a dozen Suhlik ships in the air above it and no doubt quite a few ground forces too. It was a full-blown battle when they arrived, but still, the Mahdfel numbers were higher and Kraev wasn't worried.

"Getting ready to enter the battle," he told everyone over the comms system. They all had small earpieces inserted so that any noise of the fighting wouldn't stop them from speaking to each other. "Brace yourselves."

Delyn, on the weapons, sat ramrod in his seat awaiting instructions.

Although Kraev wasn't technically the *captain* of the ship, it normally made the most sense for the pilot to delegate because he knew where the ship was going and he could tell people that so that they'd know how to work around it. It was much harder to suddenly change a ship's course because the weapon's expert had loosed a missile than it was to loose a missile in response to the ship's change of course.

More than anything, it was a dialogue.

"I'm going in from the left," Kraev said. "Can we do anything about that right-hand ship? It's a bit larger. It'll have an important commander onboard most likely."

Cynto, who was on the comms, relayed this to their own commander. The Warlord was on his own ship on the outskirts of the battle with a team of logisticians who would be tracking everything that was happening and getting ready to let the fleet know of any sudden changes in the battle that might affect it.

It was a complicated operation when they were in outright battle like this. The Warlord was responsible for coordinating both ground troops and the fleet, and that meant a specialist team of people who could process the information well and feed it to him in a way that allowed him to give effective commands. They then had to be able to get those commands back to the relevant people.

With their previous Warlord, they'd had a lot of practice at such things, but their current Warlord had only been on the job for a year and he was still unused to the high-paced environment of a full-on battle. Kraev hoped that wouldn't make or break them today.

"Getting ready to launch missiles at target," Delyn said.

"Fire at will," Kraev replied. "I'm bringing the ship in real close soon. We can use the close-range guns."

"I can see a hole in her defenses," called Gryp, who was working their logistics. "If we can come in close to the left-hand side, there's a damaged shield generator that we might be able to take out."

From the engineering bay, Zevyk replied, "They've got heavier artillery on that side of the ship though. We have to be careful bringing her in too close."

Kraev only had a few moments to process all this information and make a call at the speed he was currently going, but he knew almost immediately what he was going to do.

"I'm going in close," he said. "We're going to take out that faulty shield generator. Zevyk, can you keep the shields operational for long enough, and Delyn, can you take out that shield generator quickly enough to start defending us with the weapons when the shield can't take any more hits?"

"Yes, sir!" Delyn responded.

"Yes, brother," Zevyk replied.

The sudden turn of the ship to go in close to the larger Suhlik warship pushed them all back into their seats, but it wasn't fast enough that it would do them any damage. He was staying way out of that limit for such close-quarter fighting.

The impact of the Suhlik ships' guns on their ship was immediate, and Kraev tightened his grip on the joystick, ready to pull them back if it all went wrong, but the rounds weren't piercing the hull.

"Enemy shield generator down!" Delyn cried over the barrage. Kraev could only hear the words in his earpiece now, rather than in the cabin itself. "Changing focus to that bastard gun."

"Our own shields aren't going to hold for much longer," Zevyk replied, and it was obvious from his breathing that he'd unstrapped and was moving toward something. "One generator is damaged, but I should have it back in action before we're taking on another ship."

Kraev continued to maneuver his smaller ship around the big one, weapons loosing missiles at the now shieldless Suhlik vessel. He could see from his screens the holes that were being cast in the side of the ship, and he could also see that the lizards were firing back for all they were worth.

As much as he and Zevyk made a good team, it was always a little bit difficult for him to work with his brother. Some part of him always wanted to turn the ship around, to make risky decisions because it would mean that Zevyk, who was on the outside of the ship welding pieces of shield generator back together, would be as far out of the firing line as possible.

But that was just one of the things that came with being a pilot and of getting to live in the same clan as his brother. Sometimes, he had to make decisions that put Zevyk in more risk, but were good for the team in general, or the planet in general.

He'd come to terms with it when it was Zevyk. They'd both had to make decisions like that in the past.

It was when it came to Olivia that he still hadn't made his peace with it.

At least she would never be hanging off the side of a ship he was flying. He hoped that them fleeing the Suhlik would be the closest she ever came to being in real danger again.

"We've got it!" Gryp called. "I can see it. The Suhlik ship's about to blow. We need to get out of here, and fast."

Kraev's heart leaped. "Zevyk, you need to get back inside," he instructed, turning the ship and shooting away from the wreck as quickly as he could.

His speed was limited because if he accelerated much harder, he would crush Zevyk, who was still tethered to the outside of the ship. But they were still well within shrapnel range right now.

"I can't," Zevyk said after a moment, his voice sounding strained. "I need to finish this repair, otherwise the shrapnel will tear up the ship. It could blow the power generator, or go through someone on the bridge."

Kraev's heartrate increased at his words. "We don't have time for that," he gritted. "The ship is going to break up any second." He could already see through the cameras that fires were breaking out inside the Suhlik ship. It was getting ready to burst, and Zevyk would die in the initial blast at this range, never mind shrapnel.

Zevyk was silent, and Kraev knew that the engineer was concentrating on his work.

It left Kraev in an uncomfortable position. He could blast the ship full acceleration away from the wreck and get them the best chance of surviving any incoming shrapnel. But that would mean guaranteed death for Zevyk and he just couldn't bring himself to do it.

He switched windows on his screen for just a second and saw the red alert on the shield generator that Zevyk was working on. It was still down.

"I'm estimating thirty seconds until explosion," Gryp said, his voice strained. He too knew the odds they were facing.

"Zevyk, get back in the ship right now," Kraev said, and when there was still no reply, he raised his voice to a shout. "Get back in the ship! I need to accelerate and I refuse to be the reason that you die. Zevyk!"

But his time was gone. Kraev looked in the monitor in front of him and saw the ship they'd destroyed exploding. He braced himself for the impact of the shrapnel slicing through the undefended walls of their ship, but it never came.

Zevyk's laugh did come, though. "You have so little faith in me, Kraev," he said. "The shield generator is back up and I'm safe and sound inside the ship. We're good to keep going."

Kraev deflated in relief, his hold on the joystick going slack for a moment. Zevyk was okay. They were all okay.

Now, it was time to go and destroy some more Suhlik ships.

He gripped the joystick harder again and steered back into the battle. The rest of the fight wasn't so stressful. They outnumbered the Suhlik ships and with the destroying of the large one, they easily had an advantage over the remaining fleet. Communication was good between ships, and multiple times, Kraev fell in line with another ship to attack in sync.

He grinned as he chased a straggling ship away from the battle, Delyn sending missile after missile at it. He pushed their ship hard, so that it was forcing them all back into their seats with the level of G-force hitting them, but he caught it.

When they were dangerously close to the side of the ship, he instructed Delyn to loose the close-range guns and watched as it broke up, the Suhlik inside meeting a deserved end.

Then, he spun the ship on its head and sent it heading back to the teleport base at a much more reasonable speed.

Gryp, still slightly short of breath, said, "I'm sure that was unnecessary."

Kraev laughed. "Perhaps a little bit, but we didn't get to do too much high-speed maneuvering before. I was missing it." There was something exhilarating about traveling at that high speed. He was sure the Gs did something to the body that, when combined with the adrenaline of the fight, was like being on a drug that made you euphoric.

Either way, it had been the last ship and there was nothing to worry about. His battleship had been an easy match for the smaller vessel. There'd been no risk.

On comms, Cynto asked, "Are the Suhlik fleet at the teleport base completely destroyed?"

Looking on the map on his monitor, Kraev could see that it certainly appeared they were. There were no angry red dots indicating Suhlik ships.

"Confirmed, Suhlik fleet destroyed," replied one of the Warlord's unit. "Teleport base secured."

"It doesn't make sense," Kraev said with a frown, speaking on their internal channel rather than the one that looped in the Warlord's staff. "That was too easy."

"The Suhlik are overconfident," Gryp said with a huff. "We all know it. They think they're too good to lose."

"But they do lose. Regularly. They lost in their last attack and they had more men than that." An uneasiness started to settle over Kraev as he spoke. "Surely, they wouldn't attack again two days later with even less force. It doesn't make any sense."

"Perhaps they underestimated how many people they still had on the planet," Zevyk suggested. "We did a lot of good scouting work and they would have been worried about communicating with their people on the ground because our sensors might have picked it up."

Kraev made a noise of acknowledgment, but he still didn't like it.

"Maybe they've got another fleet coming," Gryp said. "Perhaps that one was just to weaken us."

"All possible," Kraev admitted, though he couldn't shake the uneasy feeling completely. "Maybe I'm giving them too much credit."

"We could wait around the teleport base just in case," Gryp said. "We haven't gotten official orders one way or another yet."

"Next movements?" Cynto asked the Warlord's team over the comms.

There was silence, which was unexpected. Normally, the Warlord's team responded straight away, even if it was just a small acknowledgment while they waited for the Warlord's orders so they could relay them.

The hair on Kraev's body stood on end. Something was wrong.

After a too-long delay, an unreasonably calm voice responded through the comms, "There's been an attack on the volcano base. All units to respond immediately. Defend the volcano base. I repeat, defend the volcano base."

# 19

## OLIVIA

OLIVIA WAS TRYING to retrieve her gnawed-on finger from Mito's mouth when a sudden alarm sounded in the canteen. Her whole body tensed and the hair on her skin stood up. It was just like when she'd teleported onto the planet a few days ago. Lights in the corners of the room started flashing, but this time, they were red instead of orange.

Mito started crying in her arms, reacting to the loud noises. Something akin to an explosion shook the ground.

"The Suhlik..." Naia said, her voice sounding entirely too calm. Scarily calm. Like she was holding back a torrent of emotions. "They are attacking the volcano base. We need to evacuate."

She reached out for Mito, and Olivia handed him back to his mother's arms. She mourned the loss of the child. The small weight in her arms, even if it was currently crying and screaming, had been almost reassuring.

The others in the room had already stood up and started heading at a jog toward the exit of the canteen. Olivia turned to join them.

"I need to go and get Fei," Naia said, her voice revealing the slightest bit of uncertainty. "There should have been a warrior with them in the training room, but I just... I need to make sure. I can point you in the direction you need to go in."

Olivia shook her head. "No, I'm coming with you," she replied without hesitation. There was no way that she was going to leave Naia alone when the woman had already done so much to help her. "Come on, we can get back to where he was practicing in no time."

Naia looked like she was ready to argue, but instead, she nodded. "Thank you," she said as they started to run back through the tunnels toward where Fei had been.

The ground shook beneath their feet, the fight clearly having moved dangerously close to the volcano base. Naia tried to get in touch with her son via her the communication band on her wrist, but it didn't appear to be working.

"I think the network is down," she said. "They

might have destroyed our comms towers or used some kind of signal jammer. I've lived here for years now, but I still don't know enough about technology to understand it all. It's so *alien* to me."

The thought that something could be alien to what Olivia considered an alien would have made her laugh if she didn't feel sick with anxiety.

"Has this happened before? The Suhlik attacking the volcano base?" Olivia asked.

Naia shook her head. "Not since I've lived here," she said, and the words made Olivia's heart drop. Clearly, this was a serious situation, and the concern was starting to show on Naia's face too. "It isn't the first time they've tried to mess with our communications, but I've never seen the lights flashing red."

Olivia swallowed. "Why do you think they're attacking the volcano? I thought the teleport base was their goal."

"The mines," Naia said immediately. Their footfalls echoed around the corridor as they ran, along with the cries of Mito, which weren't letting up at all. "The biggest hellstone mines are right underneath us. Maybe they've realized controlling the teleport base is not feasible and they've decided to use whatever forces they have on the planet to try to get to the mines." Her expression hardened. "Or, they're attacking just because they like to kill things and there are plenty of defenseless things inside the volcano."

A cold shiver ran down Olivia's spine and she tried to stay focused. She wished she had a way to speak to Kraev. She would have done anything to finally admit all the things she'd been thinking but had been too afraid to say. She wanted to tell him that she loved him, that he was her mate just as much as she was his. That she couldn't wait for them to start their family together.

"Fei!" Naia called, and the sharp sound of her voice startled Olivia back to the present. She didn't recognize where they were – everything looked the same – but presumably, this was around where Fei and the other children had been practicing. "Fei! Are you here?" she shouted.

"Mom?" came a scared voice from behind one of the doors. "Mom, is that you?"

"Fei," she replied, her relief evident. "It's me. Your mother. You can open the door."

The young boy opened one of the doors. He'd clearly been crying, and he was gripping the oversized spear he'd been using to practice with a cast-iron grip. Olivia immediately noticed that he was alone.

"Where are the other children?" she asked.

"They– They left with Keza," Fei whispered, seemingly on the verge of tears. "The warrior who had been training us. But I– I wanted to help. So I went back for my spear. I don't think he noticed I left." Tears started to stream down his face again. "Mom, I'm scared."

"I know. It's okay," Naia replied, embracing him in a tight hug. Mito calmed for a moment and Olivia watched the small family in silence, her eyes stinging.

She could see in Naia's face that she was terrified. Stress lines had formed around her eyes and mouth, and she kept chewing her bottom lip when she thought no one was paying attention. The ground shook again and Olivia knew that she was wishing her mate was here just as much as Olivia was.

"Where to now?" she prompted Naia. "We should get moving." She got the impression that they'd already headed in the opposite direction to where they were supposed to be evacuating from. "Wait," she said, looking into the room that Fei had come from. "That's a gym, a training room, whatever. Are there more weapons in there? Guns?"

Naia's expression turned contemplative. "Not in that one," she said. "It's for the children and only has the spears. But there are more gyms along this corridor with other weapons locked away in them."

"Can you get into any of them?" Olivia asked. "Into any of the weapons, I mean? Just in case the Suhlik actually manage to get into the base." She hoped the chances of that were slim. Naia had mentioned that there were always warriors staying behind at the base to defend it. But still, you couldn't be too careful.

Naia seemed to think the same. She stood up, holding Fei's hand. "I should be able to," she said. "They can normally be accessed by any adult with their fingerprints on record. Just in case." She shook her head sadly. "I wouldn't have even thought. You've got a better head on your shoulders than I have." She continued before Olivia had time to tell her that was nonsense. "In this one."

Inside the training gym were a number of training dummies and targets. Olivia hoped that meant there were guns locked away in the cabinet that Naia was heading toward. She opened it with her fingerprints and revealed an arsenal of small handguns.

"Perfect," Olivia breathed. At least she wouldn't feel quite so defenseless with one of these in her hand. Or two. Or maybe three, just in case. She took three. One for each hand and one tucked through her belt loop. Naia took one as well, though she didn't really have a spare hand considering she was holding both Mito and Fei.

"Can I have one?" Fei asked. He had stopped crying. The presence of his mother had seemed to calm him and he was eager to help again.

"No," Naia said sternly, shutting the cabinet again. "You're too young."

"But Mom, I know how to use it. Dad's showed me. I know." He clung to his mother's embroidered dress, his eyes wide and begging.

Naia shook her head, unrelenting. "You're too young, Fei. I won't make you do something like that. Now, come on, we need to get out of here and evacuate. We'll already be behind most people." She ushered the boy forward, but Fei dug his heels in.

"Mom, let me help! I can fight. I can protect you. I know I can."

"Fei." Naia crouched down and put her hand on her son's face. "This isn't something I'm going to argue about. I'll carry you out of here myself if I have to. Are you going to keep arguing with me about this, or are you going to come with me now and reduce our chances of running into any Suhlik?"

Fei visibly hesitated. He opened his mouth to argue some more, but then nodded. "Okay."

Naia gave him a kiss on the forehead and then they were on the move again.

Olivia's heart thudded in her chest as they moved from corridor to corridor. With every step, the ankle she'd sprained when arriving on the planet reminded her of its presence, but Olivia ignored the pain.

Her grip was painfully tight on her guns and every time they turned a corner, she expected to run straight into one of the golden monsters that had invaded her nightmares since she was a child.

But they didn't come.

Neither did any Mahdfel.

They headed toward a staircase that would take them down to the lowest floor where Naia assured her the evacuation pods were.

"They're below us," she explained as they walked. "Just small, underground crafts in a tunnel that can get us out of the other side of the volcano and away from the fighting. There's plenty of them and they run drills, so there should be one for us, even if we're late to the evacuation."

"I wonder how long it will take the warriors at the teleportation pad to get back here," Olivia asked. She had no idea how fast the ship that Kraev was flying was, or how far the teleport base actually was from the volcano. Everything was too abstract. For all she knew, it could have taken them hours to get back.

"Not long," Naia said. "They might already be back, fighting outside. That would be good. It would help the warriors who had stayed behind at the volcano to hold off the Suhlik."

Olivia's heart leaped to her throat. Kraev might be here?

It didn't seem fair that he might be so close and she was running away. Of course, it made sense, rationally and logically, but for a second, the pull to remain here so that she might see him was overwhelming.

Of course, that assumed that he'd survived the fight at the teleport base, which she couldn't confirm anyway. She thought that she would know if he was dead, that she would somehow be able to feel it, but she knew that was stupid.

"Here's the staircase," Naia said, cutting into her thoughts. "Just a few floors down and then we'll practically be at the evacuation point."

They opened the door and started rushing down the stairs. Olivia's heart pounded in her chest as she took step after quick step down the stairs. She was sure she was going to fall over and fall down with the speed they were moving at.

Voices sounded in the staircase and they all came to a sudden halt.

The doors on the floor below them opened and three Suhlik walked through.

Olivia's breath caught in her throat and, for a moment, she was completely frozen in fear. She glanced back at Naia, who likewise stood stock-still, her eyes fixed on the trio of lizards.

Catching her eye, Olivia hissed as quietly as possible, "Go. Take your kids and go back up to the next floor."

Naia shook her head, her hand letting go of Fei's and moving to the gun at her waist. Slowly, she took it in her hand and aimed at the closest Suhlik. The lizards still hadn't spotted them. They seemed to be planning on heading downstairs.

Naia's hand shook. She wasn't going to get a clean shot.

"Go," Olivia whispered, leaning closer. "Look, we'll all go. They haven't noticed us yet." She was barely audible to herself; she didn't know if Naia could actually understand anything she said.

But Naia nodded and started up the stairs. When she moved, Mito started screaming in her arms.

The Suhlik's heads immediately turned in their direction, their yellow slit eyes trained on them.

"Run!" Olivia shouted. "Think about your kids and run as fast as you can! I'll hold them off!"

She aimed her guns at the lizards, firing from

both at the end of her sentence. She hit a perfect shot with the one in her right hand, felling one of the Suhlik to the ground. The one in her left, however, went wide and hit the wall. Her wrist snapped back with a painful twist and she gasped in pain.

She'd never shot with her left hand and she immediately realized her mistake. The throwback of the gun was too much.

She ignored the pain in her wrist, realigning the gun in her right hand. She fired at the Suhlik who were now fast approaching, but again, she missed. Her mistake of trying to shoot with her left hand had cost her. The element of surprise was gone and they had easily avoided her shot.

And now, she was dead.

Two Suhlik and her, much smaller, slower, and weaker than them.

She turned on her heel and started to run.

The one consolation in all of it was that Naia and her kids were nowhere to be seen. They must have done what she'd said and fled. She prayed that she really had held the lizards off long enough to allow them to escape, at least from these two remaining monsters.

As terrified as she was, she couldn't bring herself to regret the decision. If it meant that Naia's kids got to grow up and have a family. If it meant that Naia got to live the rest of her life with her sons by her side. She would never regret laying down her life for that.

She scrambled up the stairs as fast as her legs would take her, already knowing that it wasn't going to be enough. She hadn't let go of the guns even though she knew that they wouldn't be much help against the Suhlik anymore at this point.

One of the Suhlik gripped her foot, his claws biting deep into her ankle. She screamed, shooting at the lizard in quick succession. She was relieved when blood dripped from his body and he collapsed to the ground.

But the other lizard quickly knocked the gun from her hand and grabbed her leg. Pain seared through her as he twisted her ankle. He tightened his hold and flung her backward like she was made of paper.

She slammed into the wall and then the ground, falling the height of a whole flight of stairs. A loud scream burst from her lungs and the last thing she thought of before her awareness slipped was that she hadn't bought enough time. She hadn't been strong enough. She hadn't gotten Naia and her kids enough of a head start.

She hoped desperately that she was wrong.

## 20

---

## KRAEV

KRAEV PUSHED the ship as hard as its passengers could take it. His heart pounded in his chest and his palms sweated. The ship itself could have gone twice, three times the speed that he was currently flying, but he would have passed out long before that.

It was still tempting. He needed to get back to Olivia as soon as he could.

The rest of his crew were holding onto their seat handles equally as tightly. Although Gryp and Delyn were unmated, Cynto had four children, and the oldest was out fighting himself. He had been left to defend the volcano base.

The fifteen-minute journey to the volcano seemed to take an eternity. All the while, Kraev's imagination ran wild with possibilities – every single one of them worse than the last.

They weren't even difficult things to imagine. He'd already seen Olivia pushed up against a wall with a Suhlik cracking her head and nearly making her pass out. She'd been seconds away from death and he'd witnessed all of it.

Anger coursed through his veins. That could be happening again right now and there was nothing he could do about it. He was too far out. Too far from his mate.

He should've listened to himself. He shouldn't have left her. Not now.

But it was done and she was alone in yet another base that was under attack.

How could he have let that happen? Would she even know what to do? The warning lights in the base would have started flashing, but there was no guarantee she would understand what those meant. She didn't know anyone on the base, either.

What if she headed for the hangar rather than the evacuation pods? That would be the central hub for the fighting, he was sure. She'd be walking into a sure death.

Or, she might be hunkering down in his quarters. That would be the best option. She might manage to pass beneath the radar if she just stayed in their room and didn't move. The Suhlik wouldn't have the time to go through every single room, especially not as high as the sixth floor, until after the battle was over.

He prayed that was what had happened.

"Zevyk," he said, gritting his teeth against the G-force. "Can you find Olivia on the cameras in the base?"

Zevyk had always been good with technology. Even if he didn't have strict permissions to view the camera feeds inside the base, Kraev was sure that he would find a way.

"I'm already on it, brother," Zevyk said. "Give me a moment."

Kraev waited, his heart nearly ready to burst with how fast it was beating. The Suhlik had never before managed to get near the volcano base, and now that they had, his mate was inside. The mere thought of it filled him with dread.

Zevyk was silent for a long moment, but Kraev didn't push him. He knew that when his brother found something, he would say it. Talking to him would only delay the process.

A few minutes later, Kraev's screen changed and projected the view of a camera within the volcano base.

"Do you see it?" Zevyk asked over the comms. "I found them."

*Them* were Olivia and Naia, a woman Kraev recognized by name but didn't know beyond that. There were two young children with them, most likely Naia's.

Kraev released a breath he hadn't realized he was holding. They were safe, at least for now. He could also see guns in Olivia's hands and another on her belt.

"Does she know how to fire the weapons?" Zevyk asked.

"She killed a Suhlik at the teleport base. Wounded another one," Kraev replied, pride audible in his tone. "She knows what she's doing with them."

Zevyk whistled, trying to keep the tone light even though he surely knew that Kraev felt ready to keel over with nausea. Kraev recognized that they were on the fourth floor. It was still so far away from the evacuation point. They were in grave danger.

He kept watching the screen until they got back to the hangar and he had to actually guide the ship back into the base. A few Suhlik ships attempted to stop them, but Kraev maneuvered their ship around their missiles.

Zevyk managed to isolate the cameras that were filming the evacuation pods and Cynto, too, saw his family being evacuated. His eldest son was in the middle of battle, but still alive, which eased the tension in the ship considerably.

There was no way for Kraev to keep watch when they got back to the base, but he looked at the screen one last time before disembarking to join the fight. He could guess where they were going, to a staircase that would take them down to the bottom floor and just a couple of corridors away from where the evacuation pods were.

It was a good route, and he silently sent thanks to Naia for finding Olivia and taking care of her. Using elevators in the middle of a crisis could have proven lethal for her. He would owe the Raewani woman for a lifetime if this all worked out.

The second he stepped out of the ship, gun in one hand and knife in the other, it was chaos. Mahdfel and Suhlik were fighting everywhere. Ships were firing into the hangar from above and he knew he needed to get out of there as soon as possible before one of the stray missiles hit him.

He dashed straight through the crowd, not bothering to waste the charge on his gun until one of the Suhlik looked like he was actually going to attack him. Then, he aimed and hit the bastard through the top of his thigh.

It wasn't where he'd been aiming, but it was

enough to incapacitate the lizard at least. He didn't turn around to finish the job, hoping another warrior would take care of him, and instead continued to power through the crowd of fighters, slipping past the preoccupied warriors and Suhlik.

He'd expected the corridors to be less busy when he was out of the hangar, but if anything, they were worse. There were just as many people fighting, but in the smaller space, it was far more crowded.

Stars, the Suhlik had really managed to get inside the base! The fight at the teleport had all been a ruse.

A red haze of anger filled him at the realization. The bastards would pay for this.

He tried his best to run through the corridors without being noticed by the Suhlik, but he regularly had to stop to fight the lizards.

He'd never fought as well as he did now. Adrenaline pulsed in his veins and he was fluid and flawless, easily moving from running at top pelt straight into stabbing a Suhlik in the eye and pulling his knife out before continuing to run. Kicks and shots went exactly where he wanted. There wasn't a second of hesitation because there was no *time* for that. He had to get to Olivia no matter what it took, and that meant no thinking, no second-guessing a single decision.

He must have killed or incapacitated six Suhlik

before he got out of the packed corridor and into a less populated one.

Even though there were no Suhlik here, he didn't take a minute to breathe and recover. He tried to work out how long he'd been fighting the Suhlik to get to this point. It was probably long enough that Olivia had made it to the evacuation pods. She was probably on a shuttle right now, heading as far away from the battle as it was possible to get.

He wasn't going to be satisfied until he knew for certain, though, so he still ran in that direction, taking the closest staircase down that he could. He would make sure she was safe, and if she hadn't reached the pods yet, he would guide her safely there and send her on her way. Then, he would return to the fight and force the Suhlik from the base.

Kraev's heart pounded and his tail swashed anxiously as he ran. He reached the evacuation pods without Olivia in sight, but that didn't ease his mind.

The smaller hangar wasn't busy like he imagined it had been when the alarms had first sounded. Instead, there were only a few stragglers and the warriors who were organizing the effort. Kraev hurried to one of those warriors, a male named Akren. He was the Warlord's second, and currently held a tablet recording every person who went past him to be evacuated.

"My mate," Kraev said, his voice breathless. "Has my mate been through? She's human." He didn't need to identify her beyond that. She was the only human on the planet and looked very distinctive compared to everyone else.

Akren shook his head, his brows coming together in a slight frown. "There hasn't been a human passing through here," he said.

For a moment, Kraev thought that he might pass out. His heart fell and his breath caught in his lungs as the horrifying reality hit him.

Olivia wasn't here. Olivia hadn't made it to the evacuation pods yet.

She should have been here by now, shouldn't she? Or maybe his fight had just seemed like it had taken longer than it actually had? That was possible. She might be about to round this corner any second. He would retrace the way he thought she should be coming and meet her.

Maybe one of Naia's kids had caused some trouble and delayed them a little. Maybe they'd found more people who were evacuating and stopped to help. He was sure that Olivia would have done something like that.

"Thanks," he distractedly said to Akren and headed back along the corridor to retrace Olivia's steps. He didn't see anything amiss on the way. One woman and her three kids passed him, heading to be evacuated. He nodded but didn't stop to make conversation or update them on the status of things.

His mind was a single track: there was no way he was going to stop until he saw that Olivia was okay.

But when he burst into a stairwell along her predicted path, safe was the last thing she was.

She lay sprawled on the ground floor, completely limp. A Suhlik lay beside her, equally unmoving, while another lizard bastard headed down the stairs toward her. She didn't seem to be moving at all.

His heart stopped in his chest.

They'd killed her. They'd killed his mate.

His rage was immediate and overwhelming. He could feel nothing but fury as he unholstered the gun from his waist and shot at the Suhlik approaching Olivia. It was maybe risky to shoot with him so close to her, but he didn't care.

He said something, his voice roaring in the corridors, but it echoed in his ears and he had no idea what it was. Maybe they weren't even words. He was just shouting. He knew he'd pressed the trigger more than once, even though the charge was long gone and the gun did nothing.

He discarded it on the ground, snarling at the approaching lizard that now regarded him with a vicious grin full of sharp teeth. Before, he'd been able to stay rational, to think about a plan and consider his moves. Now, he was all instinct. If he didn't give into his base rage, he would collapse on the floor beside his mate and the Suhlik would kill him in moments.

He had to rely on what came naturally to him. And what came naturally to Kraev when the bastard in front of him had just killed his mate? Rip him to pieces and inflict as much painful damage as was possible.

His tail lashed angrily. With his grip on his knives so tight he worried he'd snap the handle, he lunged for the lizard, shoving him into the wall and as far away from Olivia as he could get him. The fact that there was a Suhlik lying on the floor beside her, almost touching her, made him sick to his stomach already. There was no way he was going to let this one anywhere near her.

Tackling the Suhlik left cuts all over his body from the lizard's sharp claws and elbows, but the wounds didn't even register. In the back of his mind, something was trying to tell him that it was a stupid approach, but he didn't care. He'd done what he wanted. The Suhlik was away from his mate. The bastard was no longer hovering over her body with his mouth open and his claws ready to rip her already dead body to shreds.

Now, *he* was going to rip this Suhlik to shreds. He pulled back just as the Suhlik hit the wall and moved his blades in a flurry. He hadn't even realized he could move so fast as he plunged them again and again into the creature's chest.

The Suhlik seemed to be completely taken aback by the approach. It was so different from everything the Mahdfel had ever done before. It wasn't a sound strategy, it wasn't exploiting a Suhlik's weakness and abusing a Mahdfel's strength at all. If anything, it was the opposite.

But the pure surprise of something so different appeared to have put the creature on the back foot. This allowed Kraev to get in far more attacks than he should have done before the lizard backhanded him and send him stumbling backward.

Deep claw marks disfigured his chest and stomach, but Kraev barely noticed. He attacked as soon as the Suhlik lowered his claws, going for the neck this time. He'd wanted to pierce the thing's heart, to sink his knives into its core and feel as it beat its last beats, but he at least had enough sense to realize that was a stupid tactic.

The neck would be more than good enough.

He aimed for the chest, trying to fake the same blind rage that he'd had seconds before this slight moment of clarity, and then switched at the last second to plunge his blades into the lizard's throat instead.

The intensity of his strike meant that he practically decapitated the Suhlik, his knives going so far through the lizard's neck that they scraped against the metal wall behind it.

Kraev was breathing hard when he came back to himself, seeing the dead Suhlik and the blood covering his own hands. He wiped them hurriedly on his clothes, leaving his knives in the neck of the lizard even though he knew how irresponsible that was.

Then, he turned immediately and crouched down beside Olivia, defeated despite his victory over the Suhlik. His heart clenched painfully in his chest as he stared down at his beautiful mate, her sunlight-colored hair swept over her eyes.

He pushed the hair aside, almost afraid of what he'd see. But when a slight airflow brushed against his hand, he took a closer look at his mate.

To his surprise, her chest was rising and falling.

She was *breathing*.

He stared, unable to move, his eyes rounding in shock. He pressed a gentle hand to her breast, seeking the feel of her heartbeat. It seemed fragile beneath his hand, but it was definitely there.

His relief was so overwhelming that he almost dropped his head to her stomach and wept.

But she wasn't safe yet.

He had to pull himself together and get her out of here, or else she *would* be as dead as he'd already thought.

She was in his arms in seconds. He started running lightning speed to the medical bay.

## 21

## OLIVIA

OLIVIA KNEW SOMETHING WAS WRONG. She couldn't remember exactly what it was, but she knew that something was *seriously* wrong. Her mind was a jumble and her body had no feeling. Her eyes cracked open just a tad, but the light outside was too bright and she had to shut them again. She was briefly aware that she'd groaned, and that the arms holding her tightened around her when she did.

…Arms around her?

She was moving. She felt the jostle of the body that was carrying her now, the strong muscular arms moving her side to side and up and down though she didn't think it was intentional.

She felt relaxed in those arms. A warmth spread through her mind and body, even though her brain was foggy and she couldn't remember what had happened to her.

That meant it must have been Kraev holding her.

"Kraev," she said, barely recognizing her own voice. It sounded so faint and cracked. It sounded like some of the patients she'd had who couldn't breathe due to the Suhlik gas corroding their lungs. This jarred her eyes back open again, and this time, she managed to keep them open long enough to see his face.

He was staring back at her, his turquoise eyes wide and a little glassy. His expression looked haunted, but it was the wounds on his chest that drew her attention.

"You're bleeding," she mumbled, her stomach churning in fear. "Are you okay?"

He laughed incredulously. "Stay awake, *leani*. I'm fine. It's you that I'm worried about."

"Why?" she asked, though she knew it was bad. Everything felt like a dream. She couldn't see clearly. She couldn't feel. Somewhere in the back of her mind, she knew that she was in excruciating pain, but it just wasn't registering.

She wasn't conscious for long enough to wonder about it. Or to hear his answer.

The sound of bickering startled her awake again after what could have been any amount of time. One of the voices she would have recognized anywhere. It was Kraev. She tried to open her mouth to call to him, but nothing happened and she didn't make a sound.

"You have to heal her," Kraev said, his voice sounding harsh.

"We're in the middle of an evacuation," the other voice said, and it sounded like its owner was increasingly losing their patience. "I can't admit people to the medical bay right now, you know that. Most of the medics have already moved to the emergency medical on the evacuation pods. You should take her there and—"

"She's going to die!" Kraev erupted and it was the angriest he'd ever sounded. "You know it would take too long to get there. You need to heal her *now*."

Olivia shivered at the harshness of his voice. She didn't think she'd *actually* shivered, but it was like a shiver of the mind that would have manifested itself physically if she'd had that ability anymore.

Was she going to die?

Doctors never broke protocol. That was one of the first things you learned, otherwise you'd be sued out of your ass, and your job, if something went wrong.

"Show *me* what I need to do and I'll stay here and protect her," Kraev demanded, clearly starting to lose his patience with the doctor. "You can fuck off and evacuate and I'll do whatever it takes to keep her safe. I don't care. I just need you to show me."

The doctor paused, and then something must have happened because Kraev was moving again and she was swaying slightly in his arms.

"There's no need for that. Put her in there," the doctor said. "It'll heal her injuries and–"

The words faded into inaudible noises as something seemed to swallow her up. It took her a moment to understand that the strange zero gravity sensation she was feeling was water. She was floating in something, and it had covered her ears, stopping her from hearing the conversation going on outside.

And then what had been orange behind her eyes turned to black, and she heard the click of what must have been a lid closing over the top of her.

She panicked a little, but only because that meant Kraev was on the other side of the lid and not right beside her, holding her hand.

He'd been right there and she'd been unable to make her mouth work properly. She'd wanted to pour her heart out and explain all the things that she'd been too much of a coward to say before now. She wanted to tell him how grateful she was that he was alive, never confessing just how in love with him she was.

But she might have let that chance slip through her fingertips again.

He'd said he was willing to stay and protect whatever she'd just been lowered into. To the death.

She couldn't wait until that wasn't part of their everyday vocabulary anymore. She was looking forward to it just being them, the children they'd have, and no fear of death at all.

With that thought in her mind, a strange sense of calm filled her. The panic escaped her mind, and finally, darkness swallowed her completely.

## 22

### KRAEV

KRAEV COULDN'T KEEP STILL. He'd done that for the first day: sat with his chair to the wall beside Olivia's regen tank, keeping watch so that he'd be able to see any Suhlik that walked through the door and tried to attack his mate. He'd held his guns ready in his hands, prepared to shoot the very second that anything threatened them.

The head of medical, Dr. Zayen, hadn't evacuated. He'd obviously had no intention of doing so, considering he was still there when Kraev had shown up, but he'd quickly become busy treating the other wounded patients that came to the medical bay as the fighting started to wind down.

He'd berated each and every one of them for not going to the medical bay in the evacuation zone. He said it was safer there, but this was the first time they'd actually had to evacuate the volcano. You couldn't expect the warriors to remember that the medical bay had moved in the middle of a crisis.

The doctor seemed disgruntled by this fact, but eventually, didn't bring it up anymore. He was the only doctor present and he had his hands full. If he had an issue with the protocol, he would have to take it up with the Warlord.

The comms had gone back up at the end of the first day, and Kraev had been informed what the situation was like in the base as a whole. The Suhlik had been defeated, but there'd been heavy casualties on the Mahdfel side as well, so it wasn't a good outcome for them either.

Kraev was saddened to hear it. The last thing he wanted was to know that other people were going through what he'd thought he was about to go through. Many people would have lost their mates in this fight.

It wasn't yet certain that Kraev wouldn't lose his, either.

Olivia still lay submerged in the tank that Dr. Zayen had promised would do everything it could to heal her. He'd given Kraev a scientific explanation, but it was one that he hadn't understood or retained.

What he'd understood, however, was that while her body healed, it wasn't a guarantee that her mind would follow. She might be trapped in the tank for the rest of her life in a coma, or one day slip from the world of the living, and there was nothing he could do about it. The thought pierced his heart.

After the first day, he hadn't sat down much. He was tired – completely exhausted – but whenever he sat down, he started to drift off, and he refused to go to sleep when Olivia might wake up at any second. He wasn't going to miss that.

So, he paced around the room instead, his tail swishing anxiously. He walked back and forth in the medical bay, refusing to take his gaze off the tank that contained his mate for more than a few seconds at a time.

He couldn't stop it. Now that the Suhlik threat was practically gone – there were still a few stragglers, but organized teams were doing a full sweep of the base to root them out – there was nothing to do but wait. He wouldn't be involved in any more fights. He'd just be trapped in this room while his mate either healed or withered away.

More than once, he found himself talking to the tank. He'd rest his forehead against the wall beside it and tell Olivia stories from his childhood, or tales about how he thought their life would turn out when she recovered fully. All the plans he had for her. What it would be like when they went back to

Earth and how excited he was to meet her family. How he intended to take them to Raewan to meet his family, too.

Toward the end of the second day, the base was no longer under evacuation protocol. The medical bay suddenly got busier as some of the medics returned and the family members of the patients came to visit. Four people walked through the door and came up to Kraev. He immediately recognized them as Naia, her mate Crohn, and their children.

The Raewani woman got teary-eyed the second that she saw the tank containing Olivia and she couldn't meet Kraev's eyes as she asked how he was doing. She rested a hand on the tank for just a moment before pulling it back like she'd been burned.

"It's not your fault," Kraev said, seeing the guilt all over her face. "You didn't cause this."

"I should have stayed and fought with her. Maybe if I had, then she wouldn't be lying here like this."

Her mate squeezed her shoulders and pressed a kiss to her crown.

"You had your family to think about," Kraev said, his voice hollow despite his attempt to reassure her. "Of course, you shouldn't have stayed behind. Olivia stayed behind because she wanted to. It was her decision."

It hurt to say it, but it was true. Part of him wanted to berate Naia, to shout at her just because having someone in front of him to blame was easier than blaming the Suhlik that were now thousands of miles away.

But this was something that he loved about Olivia too. She was so kind, so selfless. She would always do something to help someone else if she could. She was going to be the perfect mother to his children, when that time came.

*If* that time came.

His heart clenched and he pushed that final thought from his mind.

"I just hope that she's going to be okay," Naia whispered.

"She's going to be just fine," Kraev said, sounding infinitely more confident than he felt. "I refuse to lose her this way."

Naia nodded, and Kraev invited them to stay for a while. He held the baby, the small mass in his arms feeling so fragile and warm and inviting. It made him even more desperate for Olivia to pull through.

If she didn't make it out of this tank, he would never have a family.

It was possible to find another match, but that was rare. Even if it happened, he would never be able to replace Olivia. He wouldn't be able to even look at another woman as a mate after her. She was his *leani*, the only woman that would ever make him feel this passionately. She was irreplaceable.

When Naia left, she gave Kraev a smile and told him to get in touch if he needed anything at all. He promised that he would, but he knew there was nothing she could do for him. There was nothing anyone could do for him until his mate woke up.

On the third day, he was really flagging. Standing made his legs ache painfully, but the second he sat down, he was asleep almost immediately. He couldn't win. He chose to stand. The pain was better than the possibility of missing Olivia waking up.

The medics had moved her to a private room with a bed and told him to get some rest.

As if he could.

A knock on the door made him jump, and that put into perspective just how tired he must have been. He hadn't noticed anyone approaching.

"It's me," Zevyk said, opening the door wider and stepping in. "I'm sorry I haven't been until now. I was assigned to the teams doing the sweep of the perimeter and this is the first second I've had free." He looked at the tank for a second and then back at Kraev. "You look terrible."

Kraev lifted one shoulder. "I don't care how I look. What's the status on the Suhlik?"

"The sweep has just been completed. The base was ridded from the Suhlik already yesterday, but now the perimeter seems clear too. Every single place in the base and around it has been checked. We're completely free of the lizards."

"Good." It was just too late. If it had been two days and seven hours ago, it would have killed the Suhlik that had flung Olivia into the wall and caused all of her injuries.

"How is she?" Zevyk asked, even though Kraev had given him the update on her status over the comms many times since the system had gone back up.

"No change," Kraev replied, his voice empty of any emotion.

Zevyk rested his hand on Kraev's arm. "She'll pull through."

"I know."

"You should get your wounds seen to."

"My wounds aren't important." His injuries from the battle still weren't completely healed and he really should have had them stitched or bandaged. They were still bleeding on occasion and would leave uglier scars if he didn't get them attended to. "I'm not leaving her."

"The doctor could come to you."

Kraev waved his brother off. "I'm not interested

in my wounds. They'll be healed in a couple of days. The medics have been busy with far worse issues, anyway."

Zevyk shook his head, clearly disapproving. "You have to sleep, at least." He came and stood opposite to Kraev, up close where he couldn't ignore his brother's worried gaze. "You're wearing yourself to the bone staying here. Just go and take a couple of hours to sleep. I'll stay here. I'll tell you if anything happens, if anything changes."

"No," Kraev said, not needing to stop and think it over even for a second. "I'm not leaving this room until Olivia comes out of the tank. I can't. I won't."

"Kraev–"

"I mean it, brother. You can't convince me otherwise."

Zevyk sighed, and Kraev could tell he'd known it was the answer he was going to get. "Then at least have something to eat." He detached a small bag that had been hooked onto his waistband and handed it to Kraev. "I went to the greenhouses before coming here. They're all fresh."

Kraev opened the bag. Zevyk had picked him fruit.

Kraev couldn't resist moving forward and embracing his brother in a tight hug. It was something neither of them had done since they were kids, but it felt right embracing his family now.

"Thank you," he said, and he hoped Zevyk knew that it wasn't just a thank you for the fruit, but a thank you for all the help that he'd been since Olivia had landed on R-2841, and even before that.

Zevyk hugged him back tightly and said, "You can always count on me."

They separated and Zevyk said his goodbyes. It was only now that Kraev realized how tired the other male looked as well. It was probably just as long since his brother had gotten a proper sleep.

Alone in the room, Kraev sat down for the first time in hours, and treated himself to the fruit in the bag. He had no idea how long it was since he'd last eaten, but it gave him the energy to at least rest his legs for a bit without falling asleep while he watched over Olivia's tank and waited for her to wake up.

She would wake up. She *had to.*

# 23

## OLIVIA

OLIVIA WOKE FEELING like she'd had a power nap.

She was completely alert, looking around at the unfamiliar room with wide eyes and a slightly elevated heart rate. A metallic ceiling greeted her above, illuminated by the warm lights that lit up the entire volcano base.

Then she saw Kraev.

He was peering over the edge of the pool of water that she now realized she was floating in. His expression was strained, but there was a hopeful glint in his turquoise eyes. When he noticed that she was awake, a slow smile spread on his face.

Olivia beamed back at him, unable to stop the big grin on her face, and flung her arms around Kraev. Her limbs were less coordinated than she'd expected, and she came horribly close to accidentally hitting him in the face, but thankfully got them to listen well enough to do what she wanted.

She hugged him close and neither of them cared that she was getting water all over him and the floor.

"Olivia…" Kraev murmured into her ear, holding her tightly in his arms.

"You're alive," she whispered, memories of what had happened before her apparent submersion in the pool coming back to her.

The Suhlik had attacked the volcano base. Kraev had been fighting. She'd been running, and she'd run into Suhlik.

Tears stung in her eyes.

They were both alive. Somehow, they'd both managed to survive.

"I can't believe you're alive," she whispered. "I can't believe *I'm* alive."

She sounded like herself again. None of the cracked, quiet whispers. It was her voice, saying the words that she'd been thinking since those fractured moments of consciousness after he'd saved her.

Then came the words that she'd been thinking for longer than she could even admit to herself. She pulled back slightly, turning to look deep into Kraev's eyes.

"I love you," she said, her voice choking up with emotion. "I love you so much, Kraev."

Her mate cupped her cheeks in his hands and pressed his forehead against hers. "Olivia, my *leani*, you mean more to me than everything else in the universe combined. You have no idea how painful it has been, sitting here and not knowing whether you'd come back to me."

A single tear fell down Olivia's cheek, but Kraev caught it with his thumb. She only now realized how tired he looked. There were deep lines around his eyes and mouth and the skin beneath his eyes was nearly navy.

But his eyes glistened with joy and love. She pressed her lips to his in a kiss that she hoped would express all the emotion she wasn't eloquent enough to put into words.

It said, *I love you* and *I'd die for you* and *waking up with you here is the best thing that could have ever happened to me*. At least, she hoped it did.

The doctor, who she hadn't even noticed before, came over as soon as they separated from their kiss.

"Yes, yes," he said, his older face a little bit pinched, though she thought she saw the hint of a smile before his exasperated expression. "You can celebrate when I've made sure that the tank has actually done its job. I'm Dr. Zayen."

Olivia turned to the doctor, but Kraev pushed his luck, giving her one more peck on the lips and a squeeze before backing off so that the doctor could examine her. He took out a flashlight and peered into her eyes when a sudden, horrifying, thought emerged in Olivia's mind.

"Wait," she said, feeling appalled at herself that she hadn't thought to ask this sooner. She'd been too wrapped up in the euphoria of seeing Kraev again. "What about Naia? And Fei and Mito? Do you know what happened to them?"

"They're all safe," Kraev said, grabbing her hands in his and squeezing them reassuringly. "They've been to visit you while you were recovering. They all managed to get to the evacuation pods unharmed."

A heavy breath escaped Olivia's lungs and her shoulders sagged in relief. She had desperately wanted them to be okay, hoping that her sacrifice had been worth it. She was lucky that she was alive to find the outcome of it, but this was the only one she would have been happy with.

She climbed out of the pool and the second the warm water was no longer surrounding her, she felt chilled. Dr. Zayen immediately offered her a towel and she took it gratefully, wrapping it around her body.

Physically, she felt fine. Dr. Zayen kept listing her injuries, which included a serious head wound, several broken ribs, and internal bleeding, and she could hardly believe it. She wondered if the doctor had kept her in the regen tank longer than was strictly necessary, because not only did she feel fine, she felt as if she'd never been injured at all.

She would have to query that with the doctor later, and give him a piece of her mind if he'd allowed Kraev to wait around in such a state when he could have quelled some of her mate's worry easily enough. It was obvious that Kraev had been at her bedside for days on end with barely any sleep or anything to eat. She forced herself not to glare at the doctor now as he confirmed that she was in perfect health.

"So, I can leave?" Olivia asked, conscious of getting Kraev back to his bed as quickly as possible so that he could finally get a good night's sleep.

She felt oddly guilty about his state right now, even though there was nothing she could have done about it, and knowing that, if she'd woken up without him right there, she would have been devastated.

Something hit her all of a sudden and she felt stupid for not having asked in the first place.

"The Suhlik… They're gone?"

"We chased them out of the base – and the planet," Kraev said. "They're never gone, but they at least shouldn't be back for a while. We did a lot of damage to their numbers… as they did to ours." He grimaced at the last part.

Olivia's heart leaped. "Is Zevyk okay?" she asked. She knew that Kraev would be absolutely devastated if something had happened to his brother, but that might be masked by the fact that she had just come out of the tank.

"He's fine," Kraev said with a slight smile. "He came to visit you too. He was worried."

Olivia smiled. "Well, no one has to worry about me anymore. I feel fine." She really did. She felt better than fine. It was like her energy had built up over the time she'd been in the tank, not expending it.

Compared to Kraev, who must have been dead on his feet, she was practically bouncing on the spot. Whatever this tank was, it was infinitely more technologically advanced than anything that they had on Earth.

Kraev wrapped his arms around her, his tail twining around her leg. She was still soaking wet, but he didn't seem to care. He held her close to his chest, looking at her like he never wanted to let go.

"You have no idea how worried I was about you."

She hugged him back and pressed a kiss to his chest. "I'm so glad we're both here and safe."

She expected a sarcastic comment from Dr.

Zayen about how they should get a room, or that this was a hospital and not the place for this, but he was just watching them with an almost affectionate smile on his face.

The Mahdfel seemed to have a different approach to public displays of affection and Olivia liked it. There was nothing wrong with telling the world that you loved someone, especially not when you'd both thought you were going to be dead just days ago.

"How long was I out?" she asked.

"Eight days," Kraev said, his voice hoarse and revealing just how exhausted he was.

"Eight days?!" Olivia's eyes widened. "No wonder I feel a bit stiff… You stayed here that entire time?" She made a noise of discontent when Kraev nodded. "Let's hurry home. We've both been here for far too long."

Dr. Zayen laughed. "It wasn't for the lack of trying to get him to go and rest up and eat something proper," he said. "I knew the attempts were futile, but we did try. I'm glad you've come out okay."

"Was that ever a doubt?" Olivia asked.

The doctor gave her a serious look that told her everything she needed to know. "It certainly was."

Olivia shivered. She couldn't believe she had been *that* close to death.

"Here," Dr. Zayen said, handing over a small bundle he'd brought into the room with the towel. "Naia brought some clothes for you to change into when you came out of the tank. I'll just give you some privacy." He turned to leave, closing the door behind him.

Kraev glanced at her and the clothes. "Do you want me to give you some privacy too?"

Olivia laughed. "Don't be ridiculous."

She changed quickly, and Kraev's gaze on her naked body as she slipped into the dry clothes made her skin prickle with heat. She definitely needed to stave off those urges for now. That wasn't the best way to keep Dr. Zayen looking affectionately at them.

"Let's go home," she said again with a smile on her lips.

*Home.* She was really starting to think of R-2841 as that. Or, well, maybe not the planet, but Kraev. Anywhere that Kraev was would be home for her.

———

WHEN THEY EMERGED into the corridor outside the medical bay, three familiar and friendly faces greeted

Olivia. Naia was there, wearing a wide smile on her face. Mito was in her arms and Fei stood beside her, a box in his hands.

"I'm so glad to see you!" Olivia said enthusiastically. "I'm glad you all got out safe."

Naia beamed back. "Thanks to you. I have no idea what would have happened if you hadn't been so selfless."

"Don't be silly. I did what anyone would have done."

Naia shook her head. "I'm happy to see you have recovered, though. We were all so worried."

"Miss Olivia, we got you a present to say thank you!" Fei stepped forward and passed her the box he was holding.

"You didn't have to do that," Olivia said, feeling a little choked up. She hadn't been expecting this at all. Saying she would stay behind while Naia and her family ran was an instinctive decision. She was right that most people would have surely done the same.

She opened the box carefully, her eyes widening ever so slightly as she took in the contents of the present.

There was a gun inside.

It had golden carvings in the butt, with deep grooves creating what looked like a bunch of flowers with big heads and small stalks. She didn't recognize the type of flower, but the carvings were clearly custom-made.

"I realize a gun isn't a good gift," Naia said hastily, "but Fei insisted."

"Every warrior should have their own weapon," Fei said resolutely, ignoring his mom's skepticism. "And you saved our lives. You're the most impressive warrior I've ever met."

Olivia did tear up at that. "It's amazing. Thank you so much."

"The flower is a *hydrangea*," Naia said, the word heavily accented. The translator didn't seem to have translated it for her. "According to the network, it is a symbol of gratitude on Earth. I hope that's correct."

It wasn't something that Olivia had ever heard before, but it didn't matter. It really was the thought that counted in this situation.

"It is," she said, wiping the tears from her eyes. "Thank you so much."

"Of course." Naia came forward and gave Olivia a gentle hug, like she was terrified of hurting her. Fei gave her a hug too, wrapping his arms around her middle since that was where he could reach given his smaller stature. She wrapped her arms tightly around both of them, only wary of squashing baby Mito, who was gurgling happily in the middle of them.

"Thank you, my friend," Naia said. "I owe you my life."

Olivia chuckled. "You don't owe me anything. I don't ever want you to feel indebted to me. And if you do, you can pay it off by cooking something for me at some point."

Naia laughed. "I suppose I can get behind that."

They parted ways after a while, promising that they would meet up and eat together when things had calmed down a bit.

Olivia and Kraev walked back to his quarters hand-in-hand, and she tried to look for signs that the corridors had been the sight of a bloody battle just days ago. There was nothing obvious that she could see. No rotting corpses, no blood on the walls or floor. Occasionally, she saw a dent in the wall that looked like it could have been from a knife or a claw grazing the metal.

"So, life just returns to normal?" she asked.

He squeezed her hand. "It does. It already has. Well, maybe not quite. People are in mourning, but generally speaking, things have gone back to normal. People have gone back to daily life, unless they can't handle that right now. We're used to Suhlik attacks, even if they're not normally this bad."

It was both sad and inspiring that life just continued as normal after such a monumental event.

They took the elevator to the sixth floor, walking past the stairwell in which Olivia had almost been killed. She thought that she would have been fine revisiting it, but Kraev was stiff as he passed the doorway.

"What actually happened?" she asked quietly as they continued toward his quarters. "I remember shooting two of them, but there was a third one. I think he hit me and... I don't remember anything after that."

"I think you fell down the stairs." Kraev swallowed, the memory clearly still fresh and painful in his mind. "I got there just as one of them was about to finish you off. I'd tracked you through the security camera network so I knew where you were heading, but I expected you to be okay. I killed the Suhlik."

She squeezed his hand reassuringly, wanting to comfort him. She wanted to stop and hug and kiss him, but decided it would be better to do those things in his apartment. Instead, she simply said, "Thank you."

"I'd do anything to protect you, *leani*. Anything." Then, he gave her a grin. "And I'm always ready to kill as many lizards as I can."

Olivia chuckled. They made it back to Kraev's apartment and he opened the door. She'd only really been in there once, and for a single night, but it really did feel like coming home. She immediately walked through to the bedroom, collapsing down onto the bed. She wasn't particularly tired, but she didn't want Kraev to do anything but sleep.

He came and lay on the bed beside her, lacing their fingers together and wrapping his tail around her. His eyes were shut in seconds, and she thought he'd passed out right then and there.

Then, he opened his eyes and asked, "Are you hungry?"

Olivia laughed. "I'm not anything. You're tired. You should go to sleep."

"If you need anything at all, I want to give it to you."

Affectionately, Olivia kissed his forehead, carefully avoiding his horns. "I need you to get some rest." She scooted up the bed and sat with her head against the headboard and patted her lap. "Lay here," she said.

Kraev did as she said, resting his head in her lap. He closed his eyes, his breathing evening out within seconds as he succumbed to sleep. Olivia ran her fingers over his face and hair, memorizing every contour of his body. She didn't want to do anything but look at him and touch him. *Her mate.*

She couldn't imagine being happier than this.

## 24

### KRAEV

KRAEV WOKE with Olivia in his arms. Despite his mate's insistence that she wasn't tired, she seemed to have fallen asleep beside him. Her back was pressed into his chest, their bodies curled around each other. Her sweet scent filled his lungs and Kraev reveled in the warmth of her body against his.

Everything felt perfect.

He caressed her with his tail, sliding it over her hips and legs. Olivia's breaths were deep and even, but after a while, he felt her begin to stir. Her eyes opened, sleepy but content as she turned over to look at him. A slow smile spread on her lips.

A sense of warmth filled Kraev, and he couldn't help but smile back at his mate. He felt completely at ease and it was like the past week had all but melted away. It was just he and his mate, waking up in bed together. This was everything he had ever wanted, and it was finally here.

"You're so beautiful," he murmured. "My *leani*."

He cupped her face in his hands and pulled her lips to his in a sweet but passionate kiss.

The kisses they'd shared since she woke up from the regen tank had been gentle and reverent, like they were both scared of breaking each other if they did anything too aggressively. This one held all the simmering heat and passion he'd felt for her ever since he saw her for the first time at the teleport base.

Their legs tangled together as their tongues entwined. His thigh wedged between hers and his cock nestled against her hip, straining against his pants. The tattoos on his skin burned bright, spreading a tingling sensation all the way through his body, from the top of his head to the end of his tail.

Olivia's hands wrapped around his neck, playing with the braid that hung down his back. Kraev kissed her again, running his hands along the soft curves of her body. He wanted to touch her everywhere; her hips, her breasts, her bottom. His hands and tail caressed every bit of her and he couldn't get enough.

She touched him back in turn, her hands curling

around his sensitive horns. It sent a jolt straight to his cock and he groaned in pleasure. Her touch turned from feather-light to hard and demanding in a second and it drove him insane.

He kissed her more aggressively now, grabbing her hip and rolling it against his crotch roughly. He ran his fingers down her side and over the curve of her breast, loving the shiver that ran along her body at his touch.

Between his thumb and forefinger, he pinched her nipple softly. She gasped, the sound sending a thrill of desire through him.

"Stars, Kraev..." Her voice was breathless. "I didn't even know it was possible to feel this good."

Kraev smiled down at her. "It's absolutely my intention to slowly drive you insane with how good I can make you feel," he teased, his mouth replacing his thumb and forefinger as he sucked on her nipple.

A breathy laugh escaped Olivia's lips. "I feel like I'm already insane," she said. "I want you inside me right now."

Her forward words nearly made Kraev lose his focus. His cock leaped to attention, more than eager to oblige. He wanted to fill her to the brim, to be as intimate as it was possible for them to be. He wanted them to come together, to feel that knowledge that she might be carrying his child after they'd finished.

But he'd made a promise and he intended to keep it.

"This time, I'm going to force myself to be patient," he replied, his hand playing with her other nipple as he started to kiss down her body.

She gasped and arched her back, digging her fingers into his shoulder as he teased her relentlessly. He kissed all the way down to the juncture between her thighs before continuing to kiss down her thigh. A shiver wracked her body and she moaned.

"Please," she said. "Kraev, I need you."

It turned him on to have her begging so sweetly, but Kraev wasn't ready to give in. The anticipation of what he knew was to come was almost unbearably good and painful at the same time. His cock ached and his tail swished in need, but he refused to let his desire overwhelm him.

He would take his time with her. Tease her. Taste her.

He buried his face between her thighs and she moaned deeply as he sucked on the little nub above her core. He wasn't sure what purpose it held, but he knew his mate liked it when he touched it, and that was enough. She spread her legs as wide as they would go and tilted her hips forward, allowing him better access.

The taste of her was divine. Sweet, just like her scent. *Amihae* fruit and spices.

She gripped his horns to keep him anchored between her thighs, pulling him firmly against her. Sparks of pleasure surged along his spine at the touch and he grunted against her flesh.

He licked and flicked her nub until she was writhing and whimpering with pleasure. He could feel her tense up beneath him, but he didn't stop. Her legs clamped around his head tightly and she screamed as she fell over the edge, her body convulsing from the power of the orgasm.

"Kraev…" she moaned as she came.

The husky sound of his name on her lips drove him wild. He gripped her hips, positioning himself at her entrance, ready to impale her.

But the memory of her small human body, fragile and broken at the bottom of a staircase, made him pause. She'd only just gotten out of the tank hours ago. Was she well enough for this?

"What are you waiting for?" Olivia asked, her voice still breathless from her orgasm. She turned to look at him when he wouldn't move. "Didn't I say I wanted you inside me?"

"You only got out of hospital hours ago," he said, worry making him frown. "I don't want to push you."

Olivia laughed. "I'm completely fine. I told you that. If anything, I'm healthier than you. You have a lot of sleep to catch up on still."

She propped herself up on her elbow and ran her fingers over his chest and down toward his achingly hard, pulsing shaft. She wrapped her hand around it, making him gasp. His gaze didn't leave hers and he swallowed thickly.

Clearly, his mate wasn't done with him.

"You almost died," he said, but the argument was weak with his mate's hand on his cock.

She leaned forward and cupped his face, resting her forehead against his. Her brown eyes sparkled with mirth. "I think that if having sex could hurt me, Dr. Zayen would have told us. I don't think he had any doubt what we'd be doing when we got home."

That did make him laugh, and he pressed his lips to hers in a gentle kiss that quickly turned fiery. He swung her legs up in a fluid motion, bringing his cock between her thighs once more. He would hate to deny his mate what they both wanted.

With one sharp thrust, he entered her to the hilt. His spur brushed against her little nub and Olivia gasped. He gripped her hips, slowly pulling out of her and then back in again. The warmth of her tight sheath around his cock felt incredible.

Her hands moved to his bottom, urging him to

move faster. When her hand wrapped around his tail, Kraev groaned. He knew it was typical for mates to entwine their tails on his birth planet, but he'd never considered his tail to be especially sensitive, just an extension of bone and cartilage. Yet, the feel of Olivia's hand on his tail made him wild with lust.

He drove into her harder, his spur hitting the nub above her core with every movement. The walls of her channel massaged his cock with every thrust and he could barely hold it back anymore.

When another orgasm neared her, she tightened around his cock and it sent him over the edge. She came with a scream, her walls pulsing around him. He groaned as he joined her, his cock throbbing as he shot jets of hot cum inside her.

His breath came out in short pants and he lay back on the bed, pulling her onto his chest, exhausted but content.

"Wow," she murmured, tracing the tattoos on his chest with her fingers.

He pressed a kiss to her forehead. "Wow, indeed."

"I'm never going to get bored of that."

Kraev grinned. "I should hope not."

She laughed and they rolled together, laying side by side instead so that she could curl into him. He held her tightly.

"I love you," she said. "More than anything."

He nuzzled her neck, inhaling her scent. "And I love you more than anything, *leani*. I never want you to be in danger again."

"As long as we both come out of the other side, I don't care what happens," she said.

He rested his hands on her stomach. "I know something that I'd definitely like to happen."

Her cheeks flushed pink. "Me too. A big family," she said, echoing his words from the first time they'd talked about it, and Kraev smiled. He knew that's what he'd always wanted, but his mate had seemed surprised by the number of children in his family.

"You're sure?" he asked.

She turned and smiled at him, her expression lighting up her entire face. "I'm sure." After a pause, she added, "I have to admit, I never thought of having so many kids, but with you… it feels right."

Kraev grinned, peppering kisses all over the back of her neck and shoulder. "You're the most perfect woman."

She giggled. "And you're the most perfect man. Isn't it a coincidence we managed to find each other?"

"It's no coincidence," he said as he gazed deep into her eyes. "It's destiny."

# 25

## OLIVIA

THEY LAY in silence for a while, just basking in each other's company.

She traced his tattoos, every once in a while asking him what a certain marking meant, just like she'd dreamed of before.

Kraev was a new experience for her in every single way. It wasn't just that he was an alien. It was that he was so passionate, committed, and intense. She didn't think it was possible for a human man to love this much, or to pour this much of himself into a single relationship.

A human would have never known from the smell of someone that they were the person they were meant to be with for the rest of their life, but Kraev had no doubts. He was completely dedicated to her and their relationship, and it meant that she didn't have to fear putting that much commitment in herself.

She was definitely that committed to him, too. She would've never seen this coming while she was still on Earth, but now, she couldn't imagine a single second spent without him, even if she knew it was unrealistic.

Olivia couldn't remember the last time she'd felt truly comfortable just sitting in the same room as someone without saying anything. She guessed it was probably with her mom or dad. That wasn't that long ago, was it?

The thought of her parents pierced her heart.

"Is there any way I could contact my family?" she asked, feeling guilty that she hadn't even considered this until now. Things had just been so hectic and high stakes that she hadn't had time to think about it yet.

"Of course." Kraev turned and reached out to the nightstand, picking up a tablet. "Here." He offered it to her. "You should be able to get through to them with this. It can connect to any planet's network, including Earth's."

Olivia's heart leaped with excitement. She took the tablet from him and immediately tried to video call her dad. Being on the other side of the galaxy meant that she had no comprehension as to what time it was back on her planet, let alone in her state, and the tablet didn't help her out there, but at least she could try.

She almost jumped into the air with joy when the call connected.

Her dad looked like he'd just gotten out of bed. His hair was tousled and he had bags under his eyes. She hoped it wasn't really in the middle of the night there.

"Olivia?" her dad said, sleep thick in his voice. At least, she thought it was sleep and not emotion. "Is that you? We've been so worried about you. You didn't call in so long… We thought that something had happened."

"Hi, Dad." She was more choked up than she'd expected to be. It hadn't hit her just how badly she missed him until he was right there on the other side of the screen from her. "Something kind of did happen. Well, it's just been hectic. There was a Suhlik attack on the base so I haven't been able to call, but I'm fine now. Everything is fine. Well, perfect really."

"Perfect?" he asked, giving her a curious look. He turned the light on in the room, and she could see that it was indeed the headboard of her parents' bed in the background. He turned next to himself, nudging her sleeping mother. "Honey, wake up. It's Olivia."

Her mom appeared on the screen a moment later, looking equally drowsy from sleep. But the second she saw Olivia, all that disappeared and her expression cleared with joy and excitement.

"Olivia? Honey, I'm so happy to see you!" Tears started to well in her mother's eyes, and Olivia could no longer hold back her own. Her vision blurred and her voice choked as she replied.

"Hi Mom," she said. "How is everything? How's Josh?"

"Wait," her dad said as he disappeared from the screen. "I'll go get your brother."

A few minutes later, her whole family was on the other side of the screen. Tears brimmed in Olivia's eyes; she was so happy to see them. She felt giddy with excitement and she couldn't stop grinning.

"Now, tell us all about it," her dad said.

"Yeah," Josh added. "How's alien life?"

Olivia laughed. Her brother was always so straight to the point.

"It's definitely been more than I was expecting," she said. "Even though it's been so messy here with the Suhlik attack, my match really is amazing. You'll never believe that the state propaganda is actually right." She smiled, warmth spreading through her as she thought about Kraev. "I feel like the most loved person in the world right now and Kraev is incredible."

"Oh, honey!" Her mom sobbed, grabbing a tissue.

Her dad was quiet for a moment and she had no idea what to expect from him.

"You sound so happy," he finally said.

Olivia beamed. "I feel happy. I miss you more than anything of course, but Kraev says that we can come and visit sometime. And, of course, now that things have calmed down, I can call you more often too. I'm really sorry I haven't before now. Oh, and you can meet Kraev. He's right here." She turned the camera slightly, catching Kraev off guard.

She only realized now that she moved the camera that he'd been staring affectionately at her rather than paying the screen any attention at all.

"Hello," he said, adjusting quickly and smiling at the family on the other side of the camera. "It's nice to meet you."

It was so awkwardly formal that it made her giggle.

Only her father raising a hand and saying, "Hello," in return made her giggle more. She was sure that they'd relax a little the more they spoke to each other. She knew that her family and Kraev would get along... when the fact that they were alien and human sunk in a bit.

She chatted to her family for nearly an hour as they prepared for work and school, talking about what had happened since being on R-2841 so far – missing out some of the parts about how she'd nearly died – and getting excited about all the new technology she'd learned about and how different things were on the planet compared to home.

It was oddly normal, getting to explain all the things she'd experienced so far to her family. None of them had ever had anything to do with the Mahdfel, so they definitely understood the awe she felt toward all the advanced technology: the food and matter replicators and intergalactic travel.

Josh especially seemed interested in all the tech gadgets, while her mother fussed over whether she had enough clothes and food on the planet. Kraev sat and listened the whole time while holding her hand, even if he didn't say much. Every once in a while, her family asked him something, and he happily replied.

Eventually, they hung up and Olivia collapsed back against Kraev, feeling comfortable in his embrace. He put the tablet back on the bedside table and wrapped his arms and tail around her waist, holding her close.

"I love it when you're happy," he whispered into her ear with a smile.

She really was. Utterly and completely happy.

# EPILOGUE

OLIVIA WAS FINALLY STARTING to get the hang of the small piece of equipment that she held in her hand. It was incredibly delicate and precise, and wildly different to anything they had on Earth. The woman in front of her had an open wound from accidentally getting in the way of her son's spear practice, and the machine sewed it up perfectly for her.

It was barely like practicing medicine anymore. She didn't feel like her Earth training had given her much of an advantage with all the new equipment she now had to learn to use; there were machines for everything here.

She would have been able to stitch the wound herself, but what was the point when the device would be able to do it without the risk of human error?

At first, she'd been scared that this would be so diluted from what she and Tammy had once dreamed of becoming that it wouldn't feel right. She'd spent a lot of time playing with the bracelet around her wrist and doubting that she was honoring the promise she'd made to her best friend so many years ago.

But then, she'd had her first real crisis to deal with. A Raewani woman had been giving birth and there had been complications. They'd needed to perform a C-section and the mother had nearly bled out. They might have solved all the problems using machines, but that had meant that just hours later, Olivia had witnessed the mother holding her newborn baby in her arms, mate at her side, with tears in her eyes and a smile on her face.

Just because she wasn't performing surgery or procedures with her own two hands didn't mean that she wasn't making a real difference to people's lives in exactly the same way as before.

She should have known that already. Kraev's face when she'd woken up from the healing tank had embodied that completely. The same medical technology had brought her back to him, and he'd definitely felt the impact of that. They both had.

Dr. Zayen caught her looking at the regen tanks from where he was reading the results on a machine, making sure that it was giving accurate readings.

"It's hard to believe that just a moon's turn ago, you were in one of those," he said.

Stars, had it already been a month? It had gone so quickly. Between her shifts at the medical bay, where Dr. Zayen had agreed to train her to become a proper Mahdfel doctor, and spending as much time in bed with Kraev as humanly possible, the month had practically flown by.

"I'm glad there's been no reason to put anyone else in one of them since then," she replied.

There had been no more Suhlik attacks in that time, though it was apparently agreed between the Warlord and some of the higher-ranked warriors on the planet that one was probably coming. The hellstone on R-2841 wasn't a resource that the Suhlik would leave alone for long.

She knew that there would be a time in the near future where all the medical knowledge she was learning would be put to the test in a high pressure, high stakes environment.

But until that point, she was enjoying the almost mundane way of life in the Mahdfel medical bay.

Just because there weren't many life-threatening illnesses within the Mahdfel population didn't mean that she was being taught to be lax, though. Dr. Zayen was a stickler for the rules, which she enjoyed. He trained her hard and always found a way to turn a situation into a training exercise, even if it was a complaint that they'd dealt with a dozen times already. She really felt like she was learning and progressing.

"I'm going to take my lunch break," Dr. Zayen said, returning the piece of equipment he'd been testing to his desk. "I want you to tell me what you think of those readings when I get back."

Olivia did as she was told, sitting at the desk and playing around with both the equipment and the readings it was putting out.

Her mind wandered, and while she was studying the readings, another machine caught her attention out of the corner of her eye. She knew what it was. It was for taking a blood sample. It would prick the end of her finger just like when she'd had her blood taken to see if she was a match for a Mahdfel.

Only now there was something else she could find out if she did a blood test.

She rested a hand on her stomach.

Maybe it was too early to check, but she'd been wondering more and more recently. With the amount of sex she and Kraev were having, she was sure it would have been almost impossible *not* to be pregnant.

Chewing on the bottom of her lip and looking over her shoulder to make sure that Dr. Zayen wasn't lurking there and judging, she went and pricked her finger.

It wasn't like taking a normal pregnancy test. This one let her know within seconds what the answer was and she held her breath only for a moment.

Her heart leaped when the results came in. She nearly regretted taking the test as soon as she had, because the result she got from the machine made the rest of her day go agonizingly slowly. She quickly busied herself with work, trying not to think about it.

At the end of her shift, Kraev came to meet her at the entrance to the medical bay as always. Normally, they just wandered along to where they could get some food and chatted about what they'd been up to.

Today, Olivia couldn't bring herself to stroll out and wave hello before standing on her tiptoes and pressing a kiss to her mate's lips.

She practically skipped over to him, and the moment she was within range, she flung herself at him. He caught her easily, laughing as he hoisted her into his arms. She wrapped her legs around his waist and his tail immediately moved to support her bottom.

"Hello," he said, placing kisses on both of her cheeks. "You look excited."

Olivia grinned. "I'm pregnant."

Kraev made a noise that sounded like a surprised grunt. "You are?" he asked, trying to rest his hand on her stomach even though their position made it incredibly awkward. "I can't believe it. Well, that's not true." A wicked but happy smile spread on his lips. "I can absolutely believe it. Of course, you're pregnant."

He kissed her deeply then, catching her off guard with the intensity of it. All the while, the wide grin remained on his face, matching hers. She looped her arms around his neck and kissed him back just as feverishly, their tongues entwining as they embraced.

"I know! I don't even know what made me do the test," she said breathlessly as she came up for air. "I just saw it and I had to know. It felt right. It felt like I would be." She was smiling so much that her cheeks ached. "And now I am. I am! I'm pregnant!"

Kraev spun her around. "This is perfect."

"You're perfect."

"We're perfect."

"Our family is perfect."

They both dissolved into giggles. It was something they'd got into the habit of saying to each other to tease, but now, there was an extra layer to add to it.

*Our family is perfect.*

She had no doubt that the words would be the truest ever spoken.

———

## THE END

ABOUT THE AUTHOR

Sonia Nova is an author of Science Fiction Romance. She loves writing about sexy, dominant alien men and the women who melt their hearts. When she is not writing, she can be found watching sci-fi movies, reading books, and dreaming of her very own alien hunk!

———

Sign up for Sonia Nova's Newsletter to be notified of exciting new releases and promotions!
www.sonianova.com/newsletter

———

www.sonianova.com

facebook.com/authorsonianova

## ARE YOU A STARR HUNTRESS?

Do you love to read sci-fi romance about strong, independent women and the sexy alien males who love them?

Starr Huntress is a coalition of the brightest Starrs in romance banding together to explore uncharted territories.

If you like your men horny – *maybe literally* – and you're equal opportunity skin color – *because who doesn't love a guy with blue or green skin?* – then join us as we dive into swashbuckling space adventure, timeless romance, and lush alien landscapes.

———

www.starrhuntress.com

facebook.com/starrhuntress

Printed in Poland
by Amazon Fulfillment
Poland Sp. z o.o., Wrocław

50831589R00179